The Central Indiana Community Foundation is proud to support this inaugural large-scale printing and distribution of *You Are Not Alone*, and is very pleased to play a role in providing this important book to schools and organizations that serve teens in Central Indiana. The courageous stories of loss, grief, and journey towards healing shared by these young authors will offer invaluable inspiration and comfort to their peers. There is great power of resilience that comes with knowing you are not alone, and this book from Brooke's Place conveys that message beautifully.

Brian Payne
President and CEO

YOU ARE NOT ALONE

Stories by Young Teens Who Have Experienced the Death of a Sibling

YOU ARE NOT ALONE

Stories by Young Teens Who Have Experienced the Death of a Sibling

A Book from Brooke's Place for Grieving Young People

Foreword by

JOHN GREEN

New York Times #1 Bestselling Author

Portland • Oregon
INKWATERPRESS.COM

Edited by Dianne Martin

Cover and interior design by Masha Shubin
Colorful Handprints © cienpies. BigStockPhoto.com

Publisher: Inkwater Press | www.inkwaterpress.com

Paperback ISBN-13 978-1-62901-621-4 | ISBN-10 1-62901-621-7
Kindle ISBN-13 978-1-62901-622-1 | ISBN-10 1-62901-622-5

1 3 5 7 9 10 8 6 4 2

DEDICATION

This special book is dedicated to the late Irene Hoffmann, the founding librarian of Brooke's Place for Grieving Young People. She believed that healing could be advanced by words, as written, read, and spoken. Irene came to program night each week to help the children and their families select the "perfect" book for them to be comforted in their grief. This book will be an important stepping stone in the grief journey of these children, and Irene would have been the first to applaud their efforts.

TABLE OF CONTENTS

OUR STORIES

ADDITIONAL INFORMATION & RESOURCES

FRIENDS AND COLLEAGUES OF BROOKE'S PLACE RESPOND TO *YOU ARE NOT ALONE*

Take a short walk with these young people as they open their hearts and share part of their journey through grief. On each page you will see promise as each of them learns to process their loss and own their story through the testament to their lost siblings. Bravo to Brooke's Place for giving them a healthy way to share their experience.

—Kim Mathis,
teacher and past Brooke's Place facilitator

The most beautiful thing about *You Are Not Alone* is the honesty with which each young person shares their story. Each author has demonstrated tremendous courage in writing about their experience. These stories are both raw and real, and I was touched by the different ways they express their memories, love, hurt, hope, and healing. The differences in these chapters serve as a powerful reminder that each person's grief journey is unique, and that there is no one right way to grieve.

—Stephanie Tebbe,
teacher at Bishop Chatard High School
and facilitator at Brooke's Place

When we experience a loss of any kind, we cannot overcome it alone. We must surround ourselves with people who love us and genuinely care about our physical, emotional, and spiritual health. There's no playbook that outlines exactly how one should overcome a loss. We have to surround ourselves with people who love and genuinely care about us, as well as people who will hold us accountable. It is very important to find things to be grateful for in the midst of dealing with tragedy. The stories of these children speak to all of this—the love, the loss, and the looking forward to a redefined life.

—Austin Hatch,
2018 keynote speaker, Brooke's Place Legacy of Hope Breakfast

It is good to see a book on this subject. Both kids and parents will benefit from hearing from siblings who have lost a brother or sister. I lost my eighteen-year-old daughter to depression by suicide five years ago. The loss of Peyton has made our family closer but has also left us with some trauma and brokenness that we need to manage individually. I have seen my three children cope in much different ways, and reading these stories makes me wonder what they each are feeling and how I can help them. I have a "new normal" constant worry for them; but I also have hope they can live life with purpose and passion, even with a broken heart. The feeling of "I'm not alone" is an effective comfort in coping with grief, and letting kids read other kids' testimonials is powerful. I applaud Brooke's Place for this book, and I am so thankful for the support they have given my family and many others who have lost family members.

—Michael Riekhof
The Peyton Riekhof Foundation for Youth Hope
www.thepeytonriekhoffoundation.com

FULL QUOTATIONS OF THOSE ABRIDGED ON THE BACK COVER

You Are Not Alone is a genuine, and authentic, look at what it is like to be a child experiencing the most complicated of losses. This book is laid out in a manner that is relatable and real to its target audience. At a time when these children feel most alone and misunderstood, and when they are trying to make sense of the confusion surrounding death, they can pick up this book and hear from their peers (not another doctor, and not another adult). This perspective is rare in the arena of grief and loss. Young readers will realize that others have also asked the questions of "why?" and "what's next?" There is great comfort in knowing that someone else out there understands. Many "someone elses" as a matter of fact. The value of that in the healing process is priceless. I will be adding this tool to the collection of books in my practice and will be recommending it to the teens I work with. Thank you to the brave young writers, and to Brooke's Place.

—Jill McMahon,
grief therapist specializing in loss to suicide
national and international speaker

You Are Not Alone makes a critical contribution to the body of literature for grieving youth. There are currently limited resources for preteens and early teens, and the stories in the book contain authentic wisdom from bereaved siblings—their perspectives are genuine, poignant, and touching. The authors of the chapters are true educators who have much to offer to other grieving young people, to those who seek to support grieving siblings, and to all professionals connected with the field of thanatology.

—Heather L. Servaty-Seib, PhD, HSPP,
psychologist and professor at Purdue University

Foreword

Warning: This book will probably make you cry. The talented young writers published here describe the searing pain of loss so absolutely that you may—as I did—break down at the heartbreak of living on when a sibling has died. This book will also make you smile as you read about the ways people honor their lost loved ones, and the warm memories they carry with them. Reading this book, I was reminded again and again that human life is vast, and that it contains many contradictions: To be a human is wonderful and terrible. Humans are so incredibly fragile and so astonishingly resilient. We are capable of extraordinary kindness, and extraordinary cruelty. The stories in this book explore those contradictions.

In her advice column "Dear Sugar," the writer Cheryl Strayed once wrote (and I'm paraphrasing here) that after someone close to you dies, it feels like everyone else is living on Planet Earth and you are living on Planet Someone I Loved Is Dead. When I was in high school, a friend of mine died, and as my friends and I drove to her funeral one cold January morning, I watched out the window as the world went on—people pumping gas, driving to work, waiting at a bus stop. Everyone else was living on Planet Earth, as if nothing had happened, while I was living on Planet My Friend Is Dead. It was a strange and disorienting place to find myself, and even though I was surrounded by people who had also loved this person, I felt very alone. I felt like I was the only person living on Planet My Friend Is Dead, because our particular friendship was ours alone, and now that she had died, it was mine alone.

These pages contain many stories of how isolating loss can be—Darius writes of the days after his brother Lamont died, "I don't like when people say they know how I feel about losing my brother, because I feel like they will never understand." No one can know your pain, not really, not all the way down.

But like so many other writers in this book, Darius also writes, "You aren't alone." And even though your grief is yours, and will never be fully understood by anyone, you *aren't* alone. You may sometimes feel like you are the only resident of Planet Someone I Love Is Dead, but you are not alone.

Anyone who lives with grief will discover points of connection in this book to their own experiences. Here were just a few that spoke to some of my experiences: In Courtney's moving essay about her brother Gunner, she discusses the terrible things some classmates have said to her, but also tells us about a wonderfully kind school counselor. R'Mon writes of his brother, "Sometimes I find myself talking to him." Ethan, who lost two siblings, writes of the crushing feeling, "Why again?" Ramon brought tears to my eyes when he wrote of his brother J.T., "He was a good brother, even when I wasn't." Emma writes, "All I could think was why. Everything leads to why."

I cried for Gabriella as she worried she would forget her brother's "laugh, his voice, his hugs," for Elijah at the portrayal of his brother as "unhuman," and for Claire's pain at imagining her future without her brother, "doing the things that Tyler will never get a chance to do." I cried for their pain, but also because their willingness to share their pain made me feel less alone in mine. Maybe different details will resonate with you, but I believe you'll finish this book reminded that you are not alone. That is not a cure for grief, of course—there is no cure. As Zareya writes with great wisdom, "Not everyone copes the same way and it's okay to feel all kinds of different emotions." And this to me points out another of great human contradictions: As this book shows, we are all different, and our losses and griefs are different. But even so, none of us is alone.

John Green

Introduction

On April 15, 1999, a rainy Thursday in Indianapolis, Indiana, a total of forty-one children, teens, young adults, and their family members gathered at St. Luke's United Methodist Church for the inaugural Brooke's Place support group program. On that night, for those children, it was OK to talk about grief, to speak the names of their loved ones, to share their fears and hopes. They were finally not alone in their grief.

As we prepare to celebrate the twentieth anniversary of Brooke's Place, we are incredibly honored by the thousands of children, teens, and young adults who have allowed us to walk their grief journey with them, who have continued to share their stories, their fears, and their hopes with us. The children who bravely share their grief stories with you in this book are among them. These amazing teen contributors show their resiliency, their strength, and the inherent value of talking about grief. And our editor, Dianne Martin, has done a tremendous job of helping our writers authentically and cohesively share their stories.

Grief comes in waves and bursts, as we are fond of saying at Brooke's Place, and it comes in many forms. We embarked on this book project as one way to share the importance of grief support to children whose lives are forever changed by their loss. If you are reading this book as a teenager who is grieving, we hope you find it to be of comfort to you and a realization that you are not alone. If you are an adult or parent reading this book, we hope it inspires you to learn more about childhood grief and ways you can make a difference in the life of a child.

Brooke's Place exists today because a dedicated mental health counselor, Pam Wright, and a core group of incredibly ambitious, introspective volunteers and donors believed that every young person deserved the opportunity to grieve in a safe, supportive, and understanding environment. We've come a long way since then, but that guiding principle remains the same. We are so grateful to all who have chosen to make a difference—from the visionary leaders who made Brooke's Place a reality, to all the incredible staff, donors, and volunteers who continue to serve grieving children in Central Indiana today.

You are loved.

Theresa Brun
Executive Director
Brooke's Place for Grieving Young People

A Note from the Editor

I love this project. These kids are remarkable. I hesitate to refer to them as "kids," because of their hard-won maturity. But the reality is, they are *young*, experiencing the shocking gravity of loss, when they should be experiencing the thrill of becoming teenagers. They are missing their siblings at a point in their lives when they need them and the comforting refuge of family most.

This book was written by and for kids. We focused on twelve- to fourteen-year-olds because these ages are wildly, unexpectedly challenging enough, with the emotional roller coaster of hormones, without also facing loss and coping with grief. The writers participated both to honor their loved ones and to help other kids who are grieving. In meeting with them, I was immediately struck by their authenticity and capacity for candid observation and self-analysis. About the pain, but also about not wanting to get stuck in the grief. They want to hold tight to their siblings—but they also want to find the strength and spirit to take their next steps in life. They want their loss to be acknowledged, but they don't want to be pitied. They don't always know how their parents are coping, but they understand it's a private matter, even within a family. Because it's private for them too.

The writers were asked to share their experience as openly as they could, and to trust that it would help someone "out there" who was experiencing something similar. Each time I received a new entry or draft, I was filled with admiration for the writer's dedication. Three worked on their own and sent their stories directly to me. Four, who didn't yet have email accounts, sent their drafts by way of their parents. Two wrote by hand and their parents sent me photos of the work, page by page. One recounted memories into a cell phone and composed via voice-to-text. It is hard to write about personal issues, and it is especially hard to write about personal grief, but they each met this challenge brilliantly.

Through the writers, I learned about the Brooke's Place facilitators—the trained volunteers who facilitate group sessions. Facilitators are adept at letting kids lead their own grief journey—and they are expert listeners. They are regarded with the affection and respect typically reserved for teachers and are sometimes referred to, by kids, as teachers.

My own experience with Brooke's Place has offered a glimpse of the gentle grace they provide for those they serve. Development and Marketing Coordinator Larissa Warne could not have been more gracious or accommodating as she acted both as my point person and the person who kept track of and executed myriad administrative details. And, at the helm, Executive Director Theresa Brun has been a beautiful example of visionary yet humble leadership, infused with intrinsic kindness.

I also have tremendous appreciation for Jerry and Linda Toomer, who proposed this project and helped bring it to fruition. They understood that siblings struggle with loss, too, and need a forum for expression. It was they who initiated this opportunity to give these strong survivors a voice and supported the undertaking to its completion.

And finally, the parents. I've been so impressed by the parents, who encouraged their children to offer honest insight and heartfelt counsel to their peers. I have the highest regard for them and the deepest respect for their "kids," who are now profoundly inspirational *authors*.

My gratitude and thanks to all.

Dianne Martin

Our Stories

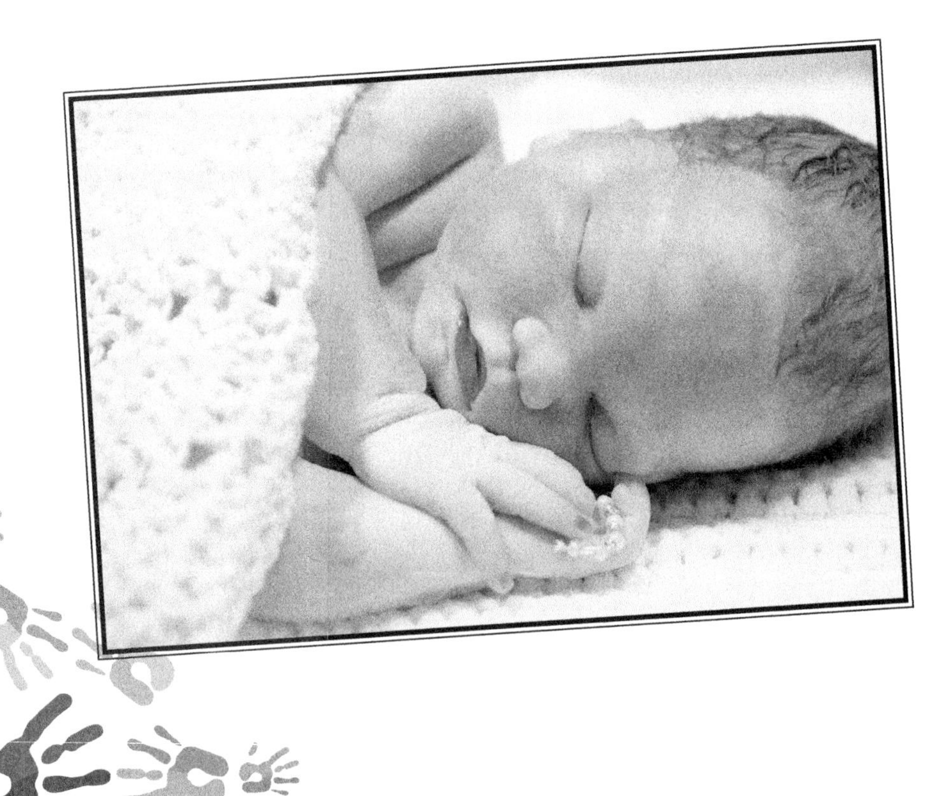

Elam

Hi, I'm Ethan. I live in Indianapolis, Indiana, and this is my account of my experience with sibling loss.

It was a summer afternoon when my little brother Elam died. We had gone to Shelbyville to buy a new car. It was a white Chrysler Town & Country. We had got it just because we were about to have a new addition to the family. At the time, there were four of us in the family. My mom and dad, Eli, who was five years old, and me. I was nine. My mom was thirty-nine weeks and four days pregnant with Elam.

We were at Sandman Brothers Chrysler dealer, when my mom told my dad that the baby wasn't moving. They scheduled an appointment at the hospital for that day. Before we went, we had lunch at the Cow Palace, one of my mom's favorite restaurants. She wasn't in that much of a hurry it felt like.

After we ate, we went straight to the hospital. My mom went into the doctor's office to do an ultrasound. It was about forty-five minutes later when she walked out with a blank look on her face. She then said, "The baby is dead." My dad immediately started crying. I started crying, too, but not like my dad. Eli wasn't crying and kept asking us why we were crying. I think he was too young to understand. We all went into the doctor's office. The doctor told us that she was sorry. My dad kept asking her why and how.

But she kept saying she doesn't know. She told my mom that she was going to deliver the baby that day. My mom immediately called my Mamaw Pam to come watch me and my brother. We rushed home, but my mamaw wasn't there yet, so we had to stay at our neighbor's house. I looked out the window as our car bolted past. I was petrified. Not too soon after, my Mamaw Pam came up to the door in tears to take us back to our house. As I walked in I saw the baby's swing. It then struck me that the life we were preparing for was not the life that we were going to have.

My papaw then told me that God takes everyone for a reason. I sat there and thought about why would God take an innocent baby? That night I stayed with my Papaw Joe while everyone else went to the hospital.

That's all I can recollect of that day.

It was at Christmastime that my mom and dad told me and Eli that we were going to have a baby brother. My mom wrapped up the ultrasound pictures and put them under the tree. We were very happy when we opened them up.

I remember when my parents told us the gender of the baby. We were in the car and my mom handed us baby-boy outfits. A third boy would be added to the family. I thought to myself, my mom and dad were probably used to this by now. They probably had no doubts that they would come home with a healthy baby boy.

I remember going to big-brother classes. These were classes that taught me and Eli how to change a baby's diapers, feed it bottles, and do CPR. We also took a class with our parents.

I remember going to the doctor with my mom to see the ultrasound as they checked the baby's vitals.

I remember helping my dad set up a baby swing in the living room.

I was so excited to have a new little brother. I thought I was going to have a new little brother. Eli was the happiest one out of everyone. He thought he was going to be a big brother, too, now.

My mom and dad thought they were going to have a new son. They spent nine months preparing.

I was in third grade, and I remember the staff at my elementary school threw a baby shower for my mom because she was PTA president. There were baby showers and all kinds of gifts.

But all for nothing. All the preparation. All the doctor appointments. All the gifts. All for nothing. We had prepared for this for nine months, all for nothing. At least that is how I feel sometimes.

The day after Elam died, we went up to the hospital to see my mom. I was very nervous and didn't know what to say or how to act.

After Elam died, people would bring all kinds of gifts and different stuff. I do not remember much after that.

I do remember the funeral though. My whole family came over. Even people I had never seen before. A lot of the Grassy Creek Elementary staff came to the funeral.

Me and Eli sat in the doorway and handed out flowers, baby blue carnations, as people came in. In the casket with Elam, there were these books that me and Eli recorded. The book I read was called *I Love You This Much*. Elam was dressed up in a *World Wrestling Entertainment* onesie that had a championship belt on it. My mom chose that onesie because my, and my little brother's, favorite thing to do was watch *WWE*, and we picked out that onesie before Elam died.

My Great-Grandpa Daniel Philpot did the ceremony. That's who Elam is named after (his middle name is Daniel). My mom decided to leave the casket closed. I never actually got to see Elam. Only my parents got to. But an organization called Now I Lay Me Down to Sleep came to take pictures. I guess it's an organization that takes pictures of babies that have passed away. The pictures were eye-opening for me. They showed me that he looked just like me and my brother. They showed me that he looked like a perfect healthy baby. It looked like nothing was wrong with him at all. After looking at the pictures it was harder to understand why God would take an innocent baby.

After Elam died, we did a number of counseling sessions.

We did counseling at Hope in Healing, through Riley. At first I thought it was pointless. But then it started really helping me in realizing that it is very hard to cope with your emotions. Counseling can be an enlightening experience. The activities that you do when you're a kid can come off as boring, but over time it gets to you and has definitely helped our whole family. It can give you a better perspective on life and why things may happen for a reason.

Another form of counseling I did was Camp Healing Tree. It has truly been what has helped me the most. It has helped me reconnect with my little brother through activities that get you involved in nature and the world around you. It is a safe environment to share your feelings and see other kids feel the same. I have been going there for more than four years, and there is no other experience that has touched me more. It has helped me push on through the challenging times that have been in my life. Through these experiences it has helped me help my friends get through their tough times.

I urge anyone who has lost someone close to them to do Camp Healing Tree and other opportunities that are presented to them. I have met many friends through Camp Healing Tree and hope to be a volunteer there one day.

After Elam died, two months and two days later, my little brother, Eli, was diagnosed with cancer. This was the point of my life when I started to think everything was falling apart.

My mom seemed very stressed during this period of time. She felt like this I think because of all the chemotherapy and doctor visits. Another reason was because of Elam's death. It affected her so much that she wasn't herself. But after Eli became cancer-free, things started turning around. Life was going.

The next spring we went on a wish trip to Give Kids the World Village, through the Indiana Children's Wish Fund. We went to Sea World, Universal Studios, and Disney World. This was really when the pain started fading away and I started to grieve better. Then, about four months later, the pain came back, as history repeated itself.

Evereli

When I was in fifth grade, about a year after we lost Elam, my mom was pregnant with my sister Evereli. I was getting off the bus and we were walking home, when she told me. I was very excited and very scared. I was scared that she might end out like Elam. That was probably my biggest fear. When my mom was pregnant with Evereli, I could tell she was scared too. We didn't go all out like we did with Elam. We stepped on the brakes a little bit.

Then, about four months later, it happened. After school, when I got off the bus, my mom told me that Evereli died. I cried the whole walk home. It was even harder because I thought God was going to give us a break after Elam died. But I was wrong. I just kept thinking to myself, why again? Why again? That day, all of my family came over to my house. It was like history was repeating itself all over again. It was like déjà vu. The pain wasn't as bad as when Elam died. But it was still there. The next day, I went with my mom to the hospital. She gave birth to Evereli very quickly. My mom was only nineteen weeks along with Evereli when she miscarried. The baby was only five inches long at birth. She also did not look like a regular baby. It was very depressing to see her like that.

I got to see Evereli only once. Whenever the doctors had to take her, I didn't want to leave her. Something inside me told me that I couldn't leave her. It still pains me to this day to think about when I had to leave her.

At that point in my life I thought everything was crashing down and my life would never be good. I thought Eli would be the only sibling I would ever have and that he would never be a big brother.

Most people do not know how much a miscarriage or a stillbirth can affect a family. Many people think that stillbirth shouldn't be counted as sibling loss. But I say otherwise. Having a stillbirth has affected my family greatly. Stillbirth losses are usually discounted. But they shouldn't be.

Whenever a kid dies, most of the time the focus is about how the parents feel. But mostly nobody knows how it feels to have sibling loss. It is hard to see your parents hurt as they have lost their child. It is hard to sit there and watch as it feels like your family is falling apart around you. All of that on top of actually losing someone. It can be hard to handle.

A lot has changed since then. It's not easy to grasp the concept of "everything happens for a reason." But I think that God takes people because of something called addition by subtraction. I think that God took Evereli and Elam because he wanted to add my twin brothers and my adopted sisters.

My parents have been participating in the foster care program. After Elam and Evereli died, they adopted two little girls, Fannie and Delilah. All our names begin with E, so we call Fannie and Delilah, who are now part of our family, Emry and Elaine.

The month after they were adopted, my mom became pregnant with twins—and last spring had the successful birth of my brothers Ean and Evan.

Our family grew from a family of four to a family of eight within months. My mom and dad, Eryn and Eric. My siblings Eli, Elaine (Delilah), Emry (Fannie), Ean, and Evan. And me.

My brother Eli is four years cancer-free.

Nowadays our family is doing very good.

While things may seem like nothing is wrong, I still often catch myself thinking deeply about what life would be like if Elam was here with us. I used to even have dreams about him. This situation gives me fears about what could happen to my and my wife's kid when I'm a grownup. Those are things that have stuck with me through this experience.

The pain will never be gone. The pit in my stomach, every time I think about Elam, will never be gone. But you have to embrace those things and celebrate the one who is gone. You have to try and keep your loved one's story alive. You can't let the pain (grief) dictate you. We celebrate Elam through pictures and things like Camp Healing Tree. He is gone but not forgotten. Still Born Yet Still Loved.

Ethan, 13

Gunner

Hi, my name is Courtney and I am twelve years old. I would like to tell you my story about me and my brother, Gunner.

Me and my brother were very close. He was thirteen when he was diagnosed with brain cancer, called DIPG—Diffuse Intrinsic Pontine Glioma—the world's worst cancer. About a week before Christmas, we were realizing that he had been walking a little bit more wobbly than normal, because he was tripping more and not walking in a straight line. So about three days before Christmas, we took him to the emergency room at Riley Hospital. They put him in a big machine, an MRI, that scanned him for three hours to see if there were any problems. For a minute it was kinda funny because the people kept putting him in a blueish dress. But the next day, we found out that he had a type of brain cancer called DIPG, and our lives would never be the same.

Me and Gunner—I also called him Bubby—were always very close. We would do all kinds of things together, like we would pick up sticks for Papaw, gather eggs, and work in the garden. We went camping a lot, and to Nitro Circus, and Mom took us to the zoo most every Friday during the summer. We are a huge Boy Scout family and did all kinds of things together for Boy Scouts, like the Pinewood Derby and cake-decorating contests.

Bub would pick on me, and I would do the same to him, and it would be pretty funny. On April Fool's Day we would prank

people. One time we were with Nana and Papaw, and Nana was coming home, and she wanted to wash her hands but didn't know that Gunner had taped the spray hose on the sink—so when she turned on the water she got sprayed, and water went everywhere! One time we went to Florida with Dad, and we would dunk each other into the ocean. Sometimes we went to Mamaw and Papaw Tom's house (my dad's parents). Me, my "twin cousin" Connor (we were born two hours apart), cousin Cody, and Gunner would play and eat supper there. We would always race each other to the ice cream freezer. I remember when we were at Nana and Papaw Mike's (my mom's parents), and me and Gunner were trying to raise the basketball goal. Gunner was tall, and when he got to the top of the ladder he would accidentally move, so it would shake—and he'd always say, "Courtney, I am not afraid of heights, I am afraid of being in motion in heights." So it was funny.

But it wasn't like that at all when the wheelchairs and surgeries came along. Gunner was in a wheelchair ever since his diagnosis. I would try to help him in any way I could. I liked to get his wheelchair out of the car and get it ready for him and push him. When he would go to physical therapy, he would have to use the machine to help him try to walk, and I would walk behind him with the wheelchair for when he had to sit back down fast. He was a really good football player, and he would love to go fishing and hunting. At first it was weird because he couldn't do as much as he used to, but eventually I got used to it and started doing as much as I could for him because I didn't know if he was going to be over it in a week or if he was gonna take a year. I didn't even know if he was going to live another year.

But there were still fun times. Mom tried to keep life as normal as possible. We still went as many places as we could. Just like when Mom and Dad took us to the Grand Canyon. Gunner didn't feel good and was in a lot of pain, but we still had fun. The best part was when we rode UTV-RZRs (off-road vehicles) through the desert and mountains for four hours in Sedona. Mom waited in the desert the whole time, worried about Gunner. He was okay and it ended up being Gunner's favorite thing he did the whole time he was sick. Mine and Dad's too. I had so much fun with Bubby that day.

We did all of Gunner's care in Cincinnati, three hours away.

Many times I stayed with Nana and Papaw while Mom and Dad were in Cincinnati with Bub. I would worry about Gunner and hope he was getting better. I had school but went over as much as I could. I always went for his surgeries. For a couple weeks Gunner wasn't doing good and had to have a major brain surgery. And that was pretty scary, but it was good because it made him do better. Me and Mom did my science fair project at the hospital, in Child Life, while Gunner was having surgery, and I got first place!

I think that that is the best hospital ever.

Gunner lived for nine months after they told us he had DIPG brain cancer. We prayed every day for a miracle and that Bubby would get better. But he just kept getting worse.

Bubby became an angel on September 15, 2017, at 3:02 a.m., and I was there by his bed. I was sad and scared, but at the same time, I was glad that he wasn't hurting and suffering anymore. And I knew he was now watching over me and my family.

The next days were busy. Mom and Dad let me help with everything and make a lot of the decisions. I got to pick out Bubby's outfit for the celebration of life and then I got to pick out and design Bubby's headstone:

I am proud of the headstone, and I go every week to visit it and make sure it looks good, and I like to decorate it too. Sometimes when me and Mom have some time in between activities, we go there or take our dinner there and eat with Bub.

After Gunner died, I was scared to go back to school. I was afraid of what everybody would say to me. But that wasn't a problem at all. My classmates made me a card each. I was afraid of what people would say, but when I got there, it was the opposite of that. When I got there, no one would talk to me because no one knew what to say, I guess. But after about two months, everyone got used to it, and they went back to normal. But then some mean kids started saying awful things. It upsets me, but they don't know what it's like to lose a brother, and I am learning to just block them out. When that happens, or if I get sad all of a sudden, I am allowed to go to the counselor's office, and she is really nice. I can talk to her if I want or sit at the table and color and do my work by myself, and that helps. Also, I have a good friend, Gabby, who listens to me and helps me get through it too.

I also started getting scared that I would get the same thing that Bubby got. DIPG. I would worry myself crazy with every little ache or pain, thinking this was going to happen to me. So Mom talked to Gunner's doctor, and she said to bring me to Cincinnati and she would talk to me about it. So my mom did. Dr. Fouladi is the best doctor. She sat with me and talked to me. She said that it is completely normal to be scared of getting cancer too. She told me how rare it was and some things I could do to keep from getting cancer in the future, like never smoking. She told me Bubby is with me all day, every day, right in my heart and watching over me. Talking to her helped me feel closer to him and let go of the worry.

Some other things that are the saddest are holidays. I really miss Gunner on holidays. Christmas was especially hard because I'm used to Gunner running in to get me and both of us going to see if Santa came. This Christmas, Bubby wasn't there to come get me. Mom and Dad are sad, too, so we just try to keep busy. Since we couldn't buy Christmas presents for Gunner, we bought presents for another little boy with brain cancer, who was one year old, and his brother, who was two. We got to take them the presents, and we did it in honor of Gunner, and it made everyone feel good. I think we are going to do that again this year.

One of the things that has helped me the most is the one thing I wanted no part of. My mom put me on a waiting list for Brooke's Place. We were on the waiting list for almost four months—which was fine with me because I insisted I wasn't going. Brooke's Place is a place for kids who have lost a brother or sister or mother or father. It is supposed to help, but I didn't need any help. All I know is I didn't want to go. When our wait was up, and Mom got the call for us to go, I was mad. I was mad at Mom for making me go to something that I didn't want to. I had an attitude and told Mom, "Fine! I will go in, but I'm not talking about anything!" Mom said I didn't have to talk. After we ate pizza, I went with the kids in my age group, and Mom went with the parents. As soon as I got back there, I realized maybe it wasn't that bad. Actually it ended up being a lot of fun. More fun than I thought it would be. They made the talking part fun. We played Jenga, and when you pull the piece of wood out for your turn, there is a question on it. My first question was, "What was your person's favorite food?" So I said Gunner's favorite food was biscuits and gravy. Then we did art and played games. They also have a volcano room. If you are upset, you can go in there and hit punching bags or hit things with pool noodles. My favorite part is having a dance competition with Randall, one of the teachers. I also like getting to remember things about Gunner and getting to talk about him. Now I can't wait to go to Brooke's Place. It is my favorite thing to do. It is every other Thursday, but I wish it was every Thursday!

We have also done a bunch of things for Gunner, like creating a mental attitude award, a scholarship, and a memorial bench at his school. We did his Eagle Scout project so he could get his Eagle Scout award. The project was a big canned-food drive. It was a huge success, and they named the food pantry after him. It will be an annual event, and I get to run some of the booths, and I get to make decisions. Now my mom is starting a foundation in Gunner's name so we can help other kids with brain cancer, and I get to look through the scholarship applications. I get to be a part of all of these things. I like being a part of everything we do for Gunner.

Every day I try to wear something to do with Gunner. I carry his ID in my lanyard, and I love to wear his football shirts and his Nike socks. It helps me feel close to Bubby.

Courtney, 12

J. T.

My little brother's name is J.T. He would always introduce himself as Joseph Tomas Randolph, even though we called him J.T. When someone new asked him his name, he would say the whole name. He wasn't formal, he just did that. He went into school and said, "My name is Joseph Tomas Randolph."

We also called him Mr. Wiggles because when he was a little baby, he would move around all the time. He was always moving, so my dad started calling him that. Our dad created a fun song for each of us that matched our personalities. For J.T. it was "They Call Him Mr. Wiggles," which was set to the tune of "Mellow Yellow" by Donovan. It went like this:

> Dad: *They call him Mr. Wiggles…*
> Me: *Why?*
> Dad: *'Cause he's a wiggling kind of guy*
> *Kind of guy*
> Dad: *They call him Mr. Wiggles*
> Me: *Why?*
> Dad: *'Cause he wiggles all the time*
> *All the time?*

Me and my brother used to have a lot of fun together. He was two years younger, but it felt like only one year. We shared a room, and he was in every memory since I remember.

He was known to wake up first. In the morning he would

wake up, go into Mom and Dad's room and ask, "Where's Monye?"—even though I was sleeping right there on the bunk above him. My parents usually said, "He's right there where you left him." He waddle-ran with his feet turned to the side, back to our room, yelling, "Monye, Monye, wake up." It was really weird because he was really fast too.

Then he would eat breakfast, but whenever someone else came downstairs, he would eat with them too—so for breakfast, he usually had four meals. He went downstairs and got Cheerios. Then I'd go eat Cheerios and he'd ask for some. Then my mom would eat and he would ask for more. Same with my dad. J.T. liked eating with the family, but he just liked eating. After all that, he was still hungry. This child had a black hole for a stomach—it was crazy. This was a normal Saturday morning for us and him.

We would play Beyblades in our room. Our favorite thing to play on was the Wii. The game we played the most was *Wii Boxing*, but we were about evenly matched. We would play with our dad, but he beat us all the time.

He and I used to play like we were fishing on the stairs. We also used to play like we were riding a bull.

Every day after church we would play with Collier and Karri, who are like our cousins. J.T. would always let us play with his toys. But when it came to food, he was stingy. Especially when it was about fries/"fwhys" and ribs/"wibs." His favorite meal. But if you asked nicely, he would give you one or two fwhys and wibs. He was a very kind person.

He was my best friend. We played all the time, and we even went to the same school for two years. When we were at school one day, me and my little brother were on the playground. He was climbing up the tan tube slide. Everyone climbed up there. Everyone had done it. So he did, he always did. He did it this time and slipped, fell, and landed on his arm. He fractured it but didn't say anything about it, for a week or two.

Then we went to Tae Kwon Do. We were doing pushups and he fell. He couldn't do them. My dad asked what was wrong and he said, "Nothing's wrong, I'm okay." He started doing pushups again and fell, and my dad asked again. My dad started helping him, and he fell again. My dad said, "What's wrong?" He said, "Nothing." My dad said, "We are going to the doctor to see if anything is wrong." He said, "No, nothing's wrong, nothing's wrong!"

Next day, we went to the doctor, and she knocked on J.T.'s arm with this tool and asked if it hurt. He flinched and told her no it didn't hurt, but his face said different. They did X-rays, and the doctor said J.T. fractured his arm. My dad asked again if it hurt, and J.T. finally said yeah it hurt. My dad asked, "Why didn't you tell us?" J.T. said, "Because I didn't want to go to the doctor and have a shot." We laughed. He fractured his arm, but he wasn't about to get a shot!

They put his arm in a sling, then he wore that for the rest of the year. It didn't slow him down at all though.

We went to our grandmas' houses often. We have two, and they both lived in Tennessee. They also lived in the same city, so it was pretty easy to see them both. The one we saw most was my mom's mom. We would stay with her and go see my dad's mom too.

Since my grandmas lived in a different state, on the way there, me and my brother would play on the DSs. We would always play on those—they were our favorite things when we were younger. Our favorite game was *Sonic SEGA Racing*. But we also liked to play *Mario Kart*.

In 2012, when I was seven and J.T. was five and a half, we were on our way to see both grandmas for Mother's Day. We were going to go see Grandma Betty, my dad's mom, first, then go to Grandmommy White's and spend the night there. But on the way we were in a car wreck, and J.T. died. That's all I want to say about the accident because I don't like talking about it.

I don't get sad anymore. I don't know why. I try to remember good things. J.T.'s favorite song was "Peanut Butter Jelly Time!" by The Buckwheat Boyz. His voice got all high when he sang it:

> *It's peanut butter jelly time! ...*
> *Peanut butter jelly!*
> *Peanut butter jelly!*

Peanut butter jelly! ...
Peanut butter jelly with a baseball bat!

You repeat as you dance around and sing along at the top of your lungs. J.T. would dance all over. It was different each time. He would walk around singing it all the time. The YouTube video had a dancing banana.

When J.T. died, the teacher turned on "Peanut Butter Jelly Time!" and I came in the classroom, and the whole class started singing it. It was funny.

My little sister, Amelia, was born three years after J.T.'s passing. Having Amelia around helps some because she is just like him, except he wasn't as annoying. The age difference makes it different with her. She's always messing around and always moving, just like him. Her face, she looks exactly like him. He was happy like she is all the time.

He was a good brother, even when I wasn't. I don't like talking about the car accident, but I don't get sad talking about J.T. I guess it is just all good memories of him. We still talk about him all the time, like he's here. I wouldn't know what to do if I didn't.

If you talk about it, it helps a lot. If you don't, you get sad real fast. If you meet someone else, they won't know who he is, and you will break down, and they won't know why or who you are missing. It helps to be around kids who have lost someone too.

Brooke's Place was cool. At first, I didn't really want to go there. Who wants to go to a place for grieving kids? It didn't sound like a lot of fun. But over time, I felt like I liked it. I went regularly and started looking forward to going and playing in the gym...exactly what you'd do normally, hanging with friends. I also liked the volcano room, which is sort of like a room where you can let everything go...really a room with mats on the walls. They have some long swimming pool noodles that you can use to play-fight. Well, I don't know if that is what you're supposed to do with them, but that's what we did with them. After a while, it just felt normal being in Brooke's Place. Everybody in my group lost somebody, and I felt close enough to them to tell my story. I hope my story helps others.

The day J.T. died, my Grandma Betty, my dad's mom, died, too, from a heart attack—when she heard about him dying. I lost her that day too. We were always over there. She made the best pie, chess pie. She made some awesome brownies and cookies and the fried chicken, OOOHHH. J.T. liked it all, but he liked any kind of food.

J.T. would have been a food critic or a comedian when he was older. He'd be a grocery store manager. He'd be that dude who was cool with everybody. If you didn't have enough money for your food, he'd help you pay for it. Or he'd be a comedian. He was funny like that. He was like my friend Kaiden and me mixed together. He was like Kaiden in that he was funny and loved to eat, but he was hyper like me. But, he was different than me because he was super helpful to everyone.

I have all kinds of siblings now: my little sister Amelia, and also my best friends Caleb, Kaiden, Collier, Karrington, and Brooklynn. We've grown up together, and they are all my siblings now. It helps having really close friends like that.

Ramon, 12

Jonny

My brother Jonathan was the oldest of the four of us. He was only seventeen when he passed away. He was in his high school marching band and played the trombone. He also worked at Kroger. He liked to play sports outside, play video games, and hang out with his friends.

Jonny always tried to be patient with everyone, including me, our younger brother, and our little sister, and he would usually hang out with us. My brother was thinking about what college to go to, like every other high school kid. My family and I all think he would've gone to Purdue if he had had the blessing of going to college.

Jonny was the person you could go and talk to. You always felt comfortable talking to him and you never had to worry about him telling anyone. You didn't ever have to worry about what he was doing or where he was because he was such a responsible and respectful person. But when the date of April 6th came around, everyone wanted to know who was where.

On April 6th, 2016, everything changed.

It was roughly 8:00 p.m. and my mom looked worried. We hadn't seen Jonny for a couple hours. He had gone to Kroger to return a DVD, but it was obvious my mom knew something was up. Time went by and the doorbell rang. It was three police officers. Immediately my mom started crying. I had no idea what was happening. I thought something was going to happen to my mom. Two of the officers took her somewhere. Turns out she left the house and walked over to our neighbors'. My dad was out of town. One of the officers stayed and asked questions and talked to us. I started panicking and breathing heavily. Before I knew it, I had lost it. I was bawling crying knowing that my brother had died. I was pacing around the room, just saying the word *please* repeatedly. My younger brother, Ben, picked up on what was happening and started to cry. My sister, Sophie, was only six and had absolutely no idea what was happening. One of the officers told her, "Your brother got into a car crash and he didn't wake up." I don't think she realized exactly what that meant, but she started crying. My mom came back after what seemed like hours. She couldn't even talk she was crying so much. My neighbors and family rushed over. It was awful.

The officers said that Jonny was alone in his car, driving, and the roads were slick and curvy. He had died due to all the head trauma from when he hit a tree. I wished and wished it would all go away, but unfortunately it didn't. I went through a lot of denial through my brother's passing. All I could think was why. Everything leads to why. He was such a deserving kid. He was kind, smart, thoughtful, hardworking, funny, and just so much more.

The funeral and viewing were horrible. They were good services, but who in the world likes funerals or viewings.

When we got to the funeral home for the viewing, I was nervous. I was going to see Jonny for the last time for a while. I started to cry right when I saw him. He looked good but shocking at the same time. I couldn't take the fact that I never got to say goodbye because I wasn't expecting what happened at all. At the viewing, there were tons of people. Some of them were family I haven't seen more than once in my life. It was good to see them—but for the reason, it wasn't. Some of my friends came and so did a few of my previous teachers. There were so many bouquets of flowers. I was at the viewing pretty much all day. When it came time to say our final goodbyes, it was gut-wrenching. When we left I kept wanting to go back and say goodbye one more time. If only I had more time.

When we got to the church the next day for the funeral, I was just feeling blue. I didn't talk much to anybody those few days. When the hearse rolled up to the church, I didn't want to look, but then again it felt like my eyes were glued to the coffin. Everywhere the coffin went, I went. When we had to cover the coffin with the sheet, I couldn't bear it. I went back to the seats we were sitting in and cried along with many others. People from the marching band played at the funeral, which was beautiful and sad all at the same time. When we went to the burial, I still had this feeling of emptiness inside my body. There were a lot of cars coming to the burial. He was going to be buried next to a tree with wind chimes. I saw and hugged a lot of people that day. I just can't get the image of him being dead, out of my head.

Everything changed right after Jonny died.

Friends started to act different. They would almost act as though they couldn't talk to me. When they did talk to me, if they mentioned anything about their siblings, I felt kind of sad inside. My friends didn't realize how lucky they were to have all their siblings still alive. Personally, I didn't realize how lucky I was, until my brother got into a car accident.

My family was also different. My immediate family and everybody else too. I could tell there was change. We were all more grateful for not only the big things, but also the small. We saw the good in life. We took opportunities and were more careful at risks. My family did a lot more of things. We tried to spend more time together and not to miss any church.

I could sense the most change around the holidays. We were less happy than we normally were. But the holidays weren't just plain old tough, we created new traditions to remember my brother. Like on Christmas at one of my grandparents' houses, we created something called a Jonny jar. Every year, each individual family member picks one item that reminds them of Jonny.

They bring that item to my grandparents' house and put it in his stocking. Before we eat dinner, we open the stocking. Each family member passes around the stocking and pulls out their item. They explain what it is and why they chose that item. After we're done opening the Jonny stocking, we put the items in a jar that has his initials on it. It gets emotional while we open the stocking. We remember the good times, at least we try to. Sometimes I can't take it, so I go into a separate room, or I try to tune it out. I don't particularly like to cry in front of anyone. So I don't really show much emotion while we open his stocking. Sometimes I feel guilty for not crying, but I've learned that it's okay not to cry. You don't have to have the same emotions as everybody else.

After my brother passed, people wanted to help me. I wanted to accept that from them, but sometimes it was just too hard. I went to a psychiatrist once, but that didn't feel comfortable for me. I think what helps me is to talk to people with the same experiences as I have. I don't know many people who have had their sibling die. And it's different for everybody, even though they might have lost the same person. My brother, sister, and I lost the same person, but we all have very different perspectives on it. I like to hear the perspectives of others, and I also like to see what helps them.

About a year after my brother's passing, we decided to try something new. We tried out Brooke's Place. At first, I was uneasy about going. I had no idea what to expect and thought it would be weird. It turns out, it was the exact opposite. There's no pressure to talk and you always have options. They also have a wide range of age groups. They even have adult groups, so it's something your whole family could go to. Everybody there is so understanding and kind. Right from the start I figured out that it was the right fit for me.

In school there were two projects that I used to honor and feel closer to my brother.

One was writing a letter to a basketball team. This was in

sixth grade. I wrote to the Purdue boys' basketball team. I wrote about how Jonny had visited Purdue that day he died. I received back a letter, Purdue pennant, Purdue key chain, and an autographed team photo from Matt Painter, the basketball coach. I got the package on my birthday, which was special to me. I couldn't stop smiling that whole entire day. I was so happy.

In seventh grade, which is my current grade, we wrote narratives. I chose to write mine about my experience with losing my brother. I wasn't sure if I could do it. This being emotional. I decided to go for it. I had an opportunity and I was going to take it. I ended up calling the book "Living After Losing." That title really stuck and pretty much summed it up. I couldn't think of another easy way to get my story out, without letting the whole world know. I wanted to let people know that that's what I'm going through, and that many others are, too, but I didn't want everyone in school to know.

While I was writing it, in class, I realized that some parts were more difficult to write than others. Some parts made me tear up a little bit. Which I was expecting, but I didn't like to show that I had tears in my eyes, so I usually had my eyes faced to the assignment as I worked. I was nervous writing it because I didn't know what people would think. I also didn't know if I would have to share it in class or not.

I ended up having to read my book in front of the class. In my head I was anxious. I think I might have been shaking a little bit. All the other books were happy, but mine wasn't at all. While I was reading I got a little choked up. I was worried that I was going to start crying in front of everyone, which wouldn't exactly be embarrassing, but it would be weird. After reading it I was happy with my results. I got an A, and I felt like people were almost touched after listening to my story. It felt good to get it off my chest. It was weighing me down. If you don't know what that feeling is, it's like if you're waiting to see your test score. But I didn't like how people kept coming up to me afterward, saying, "I'm sorry that happened to you." It makes the whole thing worse. But how would they know that.

When people ask if I could go back to any time, what would it be, I would tell them I would stop Jonny from getting in that car. Except I don't tell them that. I wish I did, but I don't. It's just not that easy to say. Everything is harder. That's what it is. Harder. Like if we go to a restaurant and they ask you how many, you'd think that would be a simple question, but for my family, it's not. When my mom or dad says "five," it's like the number 5 shoots a pain through me. Life is so much more complicated without my brother.

I never thought I would have to go through this, and I hope no one ever has to deal with what I've gone through. If I could say something to sum up life, it would be this: Life is short, so live it to the fullest.

I'm going to make sure that I make the best of everything I have because, unfortunately, for many, lives are cut tragically short. After my brother died, I made sure that I was always giving 100 percent. I gave my best effort. I had to do it. People would say, "take it easy" or "take a break," but I tuned that out. I'm going to do it until I do it well. Jonny always gave it his all. I want to commemorate him for that. I want to continue to share his legacy of hard work and determination. When he passed, I had to take over the oldest-sibling duties, which is more challenging than I thought it was. We never realized how much he helped us.

Sometimes I wonder what it would be like if he were still here. Things would be a lot different. I could tell people all my siblings were alive, and some friendships would be different. I really wish Jonny were still here because I just really need him. Sometimes I think to myself about some of the good things that have happened since his passing. For me it's tough to admit that there are good things that have happened. I feel kind of empty without him. You wouldn't think you would have to go through this at this age, but it does happen. And it really stinks. Especially at this age because so much is already happening.

In this journey of denial and grieving, people have told me that it would get easier. The truth is, it really doesn't. Although it does get easier to deal with.

Through this experience I've learned a lot. It was a tragedy, and I have decided to write a chapter for this book, for Jonny. With this, I hope to help others with their pain. I want to let other people know that they are not alone. There are others who have gone through what they have. It hurts to lose a loved one, and nothing makes it better. You need to keep their memory alive.

This was an amazing opportunity. This was a way to get it out there. To help others and to always have hope.

Emma, 12

Joseph

A little bit of background: I'm the youngest of eight, I'm an aunt of fourteen—almost fifteen—and in March 2016, I lost my twenty-one-year-old brother, Joseph, to suicide.

March 15, 2016, was a normal Tuesday. I had drama practice and was hanging out with one of my close friends. We were being common teenagers and taking selfies. It was a beautiful spring day, one of the first good-weather days after the cold winter. At the time, it seemed like one of the best days I had had that year.

My mom picked me up after drama practice. We got home, and like usual, I was happy to see my dog. I remember looking up and seeing my dad standing in the doorway. I noticed his eyes were extremely red—and me being me, I thought the worst. My grandfather had died a couple months before, and I immediately thought my grandmother had died. To be completely honest with myself, that is not the worst. No matter how much I love my grandmother, what followed was much worse. As I walked in the door, my dad told me to go to the dining room, which was weird, and looking back, I know it was so he could explain to my mother what was going on because she was as out of the loop as I was. I started walking, and to get to the dining room, I had to walk through the kitchen, where my brother Michael was staring out the glass door with his hands on his hips. Michael is my oldest sibling. He and I are almost exactly twenty years apart, to give you an idea. At the time, he was thirty-two and I was twelve. I kept walking towards the dining room, but ended up dropping my bag and asking him what was going on. By this time we were face to face, and he told me, "Joseph shot himself." My mind was racing and I couldn't think straight. Coincidentally, my sister Leah, who is the fourth child, came over to give us thank you cards, as earlier that week was my nephew's birthday. And, at the same time, my brother Matthias's bus arrived home. He's three years older than I am, but he had just had his sixteenth birthday two days before. He was walking up the driveway as my dad was asking my sister to get out of the car. She jokingly responded with, "I'm not getting out, you come here." Of course, she didn't know, and when my dad asked again, a little more intense, she realized something was wrong. She and Matthias were told together, and they both came inside. I remember earlier that week, earlier that year, really whenever I asked Matthias for a hug, he wouldn't hug me, but that day, that day he did. I remember that feeling, and as I'm writing this, I can still feel it in the bottom of my stomach. A feeling I wish on no one.

Later that night, my parents had to go down to Bloomington to get Joseph's stuff, so I went home with my sister. While in her car, she was explaining to her husband what had happened. That was when I realized that my brother was dead. She used the word *suicide*, which made me think, "doesn't that mean he's dead?" The answer is yes. And I didn't know that...that he was dead.... I thought he was in the hospital or something. I didn't want to upset my sister any further so I kept it to myself, but I couldn't hold back the tears from the realization.

I went all over the place that day, from Leah's house—where I texted my friends, telling them I wouldn't be at school the next day and why—to my oldest sister Laura's, then to my oldest brother's, then home. It was hard, and I didn't know what to do. I didn't understand what I was feeling. I know now it was a mix of emotion, because I was heartbroken—yet also managing to have moments of fun. But for the longest time, it felt wrong to be happy, so instead, I allowed myself to feel only sad. Please don't do that to yourself. It isn't healthy, and it doesn't help. It is okay to laugh and be happy, I promise.

Allow me to share a memory.

Three months earlier, Christmas break 2015, my family went out for dinner. Before leaving, my dad insisted Joseph and I take a picture together in front of the tree by our house—such an odd request, causing both Joseph and me to make weird faces during the photo. Sarcastic sibling love faces. While taking the picture, my dad made a comment about how I was wearing black on black, that I didn't look good and should go change. Looking back on it, he was right, but I was stubborn. During this, Joseph was writing on a small piece of paper, but I didn't think anything of it at the time. Later, as we were getting into the car, Joe handed me a piece of paper. At first I thought it was just a piece of trash, but excitement got the better of me, and I opened it. To my surprise I found a small note. It said, "You are beautiful." I've been told this many times, but until that moment, I didn't believe anyone. He's the only person I have ever believed. I still have the photo of us, but sadly I don't have the note.

My brother—all my brothers—have always been there for me, and in that way, I am exceptionally lucky.

I have another story to share, only one more, but one that is significant to me. This one took place fall break 2014, I believe.

We were on a walk…my parents, my oldest brother and his wife and son (Jen and Quinn), and my brothers Matthias and Joseph, and I. As usual, someone teased me, and I got upset, so I ran up the trail so I didn't have to walk with them. Eventually Joseph caught up to me. We walked in silence for a while, but soon enough I was talking to him about how much it annoyed me when people made fun of me. After we talked for a bit, Joseph helped me plot my revenge. We decided we'd plant barricades on the path. We used fallen trees and branches to construct three successive walls, and after each one, we could hear the rest of our group grumbling and struggling to get through them. We came out of the trail long before everyone else, sat on a bench and waited, content and pleased with ourselves, and agreed that, next time, we'd bring superglue.

Joseph was always there for me.

I remember Joseph's funeral and wake like it was last weekend. It was sad, and I was scared out of my mind. A lot of my friends came, and even a couple of my teachers. All of Joseph's friends were there, and even those who didn't know him well. We had easily a hundred cars in the funeral procession. It was beautiful. Believe me when I say that.

When the Monday after the funeral rolled around, and I knew I had to go back to school, I was a little scared everyone would judge. But when I walked into my classroom, I felt nothing but love. My friends had spent two classes making a poster. On one side of the poster, it had the lyrics of Bruno Mars's song "Count on Me," and on the other side, in big bold letters, it said, WE ARE THERE FOR YOU!

Okay, I'm done sharing my own story now.

Hopefully you have seen a few similarities as well as a lot of differences between my story and yours.

One thing I want you to know is that everyone's story is going to seem different, and maybe even easier or harder than your own struggle. No one has been through exactly what you have, and maybe someone has lost everything and you have lost "only" a sibling, but to you that is everything. Losing a sibling is a big deal. Yes, if you were to endure what some others have, that might be worse. But your worst moment has still been devastating, and it has shaken the foundation of your world.

I just had to get that out because, as I think about my grief, I know that's one challenge that seemed to always pop up. If I tried to talk to my friends about how much it hurt, I always had that one friend who had lost more people than I had and would always bring that fact up. It often made me think that I hadn't been through anything. She had lost all her grandparents. And me? All I had lost was my brother. When I think about this now, though, I honestly want to slap myself. "All" I had lost was my brother? I lost "only" my brother? No, I lost my BROTHER, one of my best friends. I lost the person who stood up for me. I lost the person I looked up to. I lost who knows how many years of my life because of grief. I can tell you right now it's been at least two years of my life, filled with grief. So, no, I didn't lose "only" one person, I lost everything. That's how it felt, and how it still feels at times.

There is so much I want to go back and tell myself, but I can't, so instead I'm telling you.

Grief is hard, and different for each grieving person. Depending on the situation—who the person lost, what age they are, who they are—everything, even the small things, changes one person's experience from another's. Both Matthias and I lost the same person—and for both of us, it was an older brother. Matthias and Joseph were very close, and Joseph and I were very close. Anyone who hasn't experienced grief might think our experience would be very similar if not the same. On the contrary, because Matthias and I aren't the same person. We each had our own personal relationship with Joseph, so the loss does not carry the exact same significance. I was Joseph's only little sister, and because of that, it felt special. Even though I was twelve and he was twenty-one, we had a tight bond. I know that in some ways his relationships with Matthias and Michael were closer than ours, but they were brothers. Joseph and I, well we were a little sister and a big brother Jo-Jo. Even with eight kids in the family, his relationship was unique, and special, with each sibling.

Each person is different—and everyone grieves differently. This is one thing that is super important to take notice of while grieving. Yes, it is good to talk to others, especially other family members or friends who lost the same person as you, but don't compare how they grieve to how you grieve. At times it's going to seem like some people in your family are done grieving, and you might feel you're the only one left who hasn't healed, but listen to me when I say that everyone is still grieving, but sometimes it's easier not to show it. Certain people will try to be the strong leader of the family, and maybe that is you. If so, allow yourself a break every once in a while. It will be good for you. If it's someone else who is being the strong leader, understand that even when they put on the brave face, they are still feeling the pain. No need to worry, everyone and everything will turn out okay, even if it doesn't seem like it.

As I write this, I find it hard at times to continue, but I keep reminding myself that it will help others. That is all I want. I want to help. Life can get tough, life can seem overwhelming, and sometimes it feels like nothing is going your way. Everyone has these feelings, not just those who are grieving. It is important that you know the world is not against you, and that even though something seems hard, if you truly believe it is for the best then you should do it.

For example, it's hard for me to talk with other people about Joseph. I tend to shove it all down and ignore what I'm feeling, at least until I'm with one of my close friends. He is the only person I tell certain thoughts to, and without him, I probably wouldn't share as much. But I promise you, with everything I have, that no matter who you turn to, if they know your situation, they will listen, and they will care. Granted, this doesn't mean go open up to the school bully (don't laugh, but that's what I did at one point), but do know it's okay to reach out to close friends, or parents. I know some of you are thinking, "My parents, yeah I love them, but sometimes it's awkward," which is totally understandable. I think a few of you might have expected me to say something like, "Go to your parents, you'll regret it," but in my experience, I haven't. Sometimes there are things you need to discuss with someone it won't affect, someone who won't get overly upset unnecessarily. That being said, parents/adult figures can be the right ones to turn to, especially when it's a matter of safety or extreme emotion, such as depression.

I just want you to feel like you can talk to whoever you want. As long as you don't hurt yourself, or anyone else, there are no rules to grief.

As I said before, I have a huge family, and with that huge family comes a lot of drama and interesting situations. It can be tough dealing with my grief when my family is around. I often forget I need to allow myself time alone. Time to grieve in silence.

But we are also all close to each other, and we always joke with each other. For as long as I can remember I have had all my siblings right next to me through everything. At my grandfather's funeral, Joseph held me close, my sister stood with me, and all my family understood me, like I understood them. I remember, at Joseph's funeral, thinking to myself, "Who is going to hold me today?" and there they were, my brothers and my sisters. We all have each other's backs, and there is no one else I would want for my siblings other than them. This whole situation makes me say "I love you" more, and hug my family more, but most importantly, it makes me remember who we were before, and who we always will be, no matter what.

Something that keeps coming up, both in this story, and in my life and mind, is the phrase that has gotten me through it all: "We are there for you." It is how I started this journey, what was before this journey, and how I get through every day in this journey. We are there for you—even if we can't talk to you, we can share our stories and experiences. Your family, they are there for you. Your friends, your animals, they are there for you. I was trying to find a creative way to end this short story of mine. At first, I couldn't think of anything, but now I can. Always remember, "There for you." Family, friends, everyone, me. I promise, it will be okay. Maybe not today or tomorrow, but it will be. Remind yourself, every day.

I'll be honest, there have been times when I've been afraid that I'll forget how my brother acted, or his laugh, his voice, his hugs, and I know I'm not the only one who has thought things like this before. But don't worry, you won't forget. The memories are deeper than normal memories. They are special. They are yours and theirs.

I still feel grief, even today, and I know that's not going away.

A couple of things that help me cope from day to day: Sometimes I need to just sit and cry, which is okay. Hot chocolate or other warm beverages also help. Sometimes I'll look at old photos and remember what happened that day. I'll occasionally talk with my friends, family, or other people I trust, about how I'm feeling. Another thing that helps at some points is being with my family, knowing they went through it, too, and that I have people who knew Joseph as well as, if not better than, I did. Also, as weird as it sounds, I love thunderstorms and snowy days, so when it's thundering or snowing I go outside and just enjoy it for five to fifteen minutes. Nature is a good way of clearing the senses, so I suggest going outside when it's your favorite type of weather.

I hope I have, in some way, helped you. Thank you for reading my story. It means a lot to me, and it helped me to write it. So once again, thank you.

Gabriella, 14

Katerina

I was nearing the end of fifth grade when I experienced my first loss of the two I'm going to tell you about.

When I first heard my mom was pregnant, I was scared. It was time again for the mystery of guessing what the baby was gonna be. A boy or a girl? I already had five siblings. One older sister and four younger brothers. I was used to having younger brothers, so I was afraid of having a younger sister.

I thought the only reason my parents loved me, especially my mom, was because I was their youngest girl, and that was the only reason they kept me around. I even remember once asking my mom what made me and my sister special, and she said because my sister was her first-born and I was her baby girl.

I spent most of my mom's pregnancy trying to forget she was so, but it was hard. It wasn't like I was going to hate the baby if it was a girl. I would have just been miserably upset and would not want to do much with her.

I would pray some nights that the baby wasn't a girl, and if it already was, to change it. Throughout the nine months, whenever we all went to the store, my dad would tease me around the baby stuff and point at the girls clothes, and when I got upset, he'd call me selfish.

One day Mom was feeling really sick, and she was pale. My dad assumed she was about to give birth, so he called the ambulance.

We went to the hospital to see my mom and waited in a waiting room for about three hours, and we didn't even get to go in and see her. We went home, but for only an hour or two, and then returned to the hospital. We went back to the waiting room once again.

When we finally were allowed in her room, my mom's eyes looked red, as if she was crying. I overheard a doctor say to her, "Sorry for your loss." We didn't get to stay for long, just a couple of minutes. Then we were sent to another room for what felt like hours. We finally went home. My grandpa came to watch us. My dad picked up Taco Bell for dinner and called us older kids upstairs. He told us that they lost the baby. Even though I kind of already knew, it hit me like new news. Even though it wasn't really important at the moment, I asked if the baby was a girl or boy, and he said girl. My parents named her Katerina, after my grandmother.

For the longest time I thought it was all my fault. I thought I killed her. I thought, because I didn't want a sister, she died, and I felt really guilty. I felt like I didn't deserve to live, and no matter how many times my mom told me I didn't do it, or it wasn't my fault, I still thought it was. It took a long time for me to realize it wasn't my fault. Even though I wasn't excited about a baby sister at first, I love her and wish she was here along with my other sister I'm going to tell you about. If I could see her now, just for a moment, I would tell her how much I love her and wish she was here and how I can't wait to meet her in heaven.

Evalyn

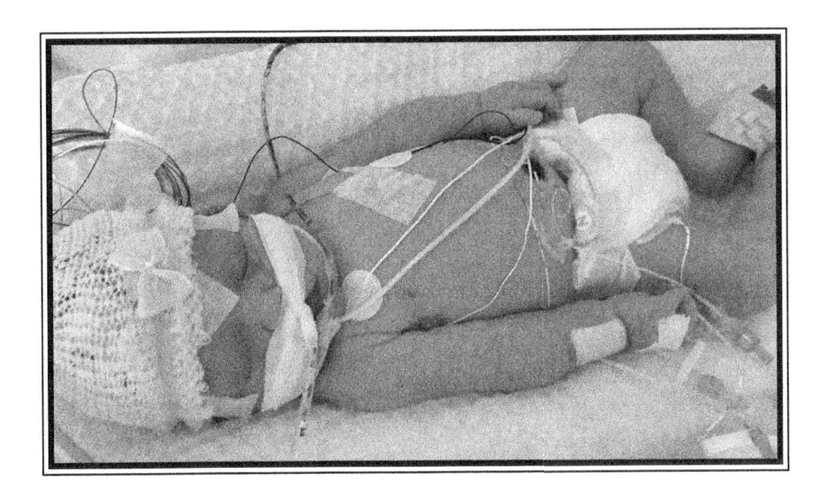

My second story happened when I was in the seventh grade. It was the worst year in my life thus far. You would think, from my last experience, I would like to have a little sister, but you'd be wrong. Though I wasn't as upset as last time, I was still pretty upset. I knew it was a girl, because my mom avoided telling me the gender of the baby and said she didn't know, but I knew she was lying. She later told me the news, but it still hit me like new news again.

She was born on July 30. I believe I visited my mom the next day. She was in the middle of watching *The Lion King*. The baby wasn't with her, and we asked where she was, and my mom said she was sick and was transferred to another hospital. I believe that was my first day of school, so I missed it. The next day, I went to school. I had a terrible first few days of school knowing my little sister was sick, but I didn't want to visit her. It was too hard, for multiple reasons. I started crying in my math class, overwhelmed with not knowing what to do. Overwhelmed with knowing she didn't have much time left. And not sure if I should go see her. My counselor came in the classroom, worried I might hurt myself or something. So we talked, and then I just sorted uniforms with her for the rest of the school day. When I got home my parents weren't there and my grandparents on both my mom's and dad's sides were. When my parents got home they said she barely had any time left, and wanted us to visit her tomorrow. I said I didn't want to go and my dad yelled at me and called me selfish. I got so upset. He had no idea what I was going through. No idea why I didn't want to go.

Deep down, I wanted to go, but it was hard. I ran to my room not knowing what to do. Angry. Angry with my dad, angry with the world, angry with me. My mom soon came up to my room to talk to me. We talked it out and I decided to go.

I wasn't as nervous as I thought I would be, and when I got to my sister's room, my mom was there with her. My sister was wearing a hat with her name, "Evalyn," printed on it. She was so tiny and beautiful, so soft and warm. She was connected to so many machines, with tubes up her nose and down her throat. My mom said she had brain damage from the lack of oxygen. I wanted to hold her, but my mom said she was too cold and needed to rest but I can hold her later. I stayed there for hours, in the room and in the cafeteria, and my mom said I could hold her tomorrow.

A couple days passed and I stayed home from school because I was sick. I asked my mom when I could go see Evalyn again and my mom said, "She died yesterday." I started crying. I was so

upset I couldn't say goodbye. Upset I didn't get to hold her, not once. Upset it turned out this way and she didn't survive. She's now inside a teddy bear in my mom's room. Well, her ashes at least. It's a teddy bear urn.

I love both of my sisters deeply, and through my experience I am now prepared/okay with having a little sister and can't wait to see them again. I've learned I don't need to be the youngest girl, to be loved, and having a younger sister won't be the end of the world, not even close.

If you're also afraid of having a younger sibling, just know you're not alone and it doesn't make you a bad person. It's new and will definitely change your life, but not necessarily in a bad way. Your family will love you no matter what and you'll always be their baby.

For the people who are going through grief, just remember you're also not alone. It's scary and sad and you're really going to miss them. Also remember not everyone copes the same way and it's okay to feel all kinds of different emotions. When I'm sad I like to think that they're in a better place and are much happier now and how someday I'll see them again. Just stay strong and keep their memory alive, because they'll always be with you in your heart.

Zareya, 13

Lamont

I found out my brother was dead April 13, 2017.

I was laying in my bed asleep late that night and my phone went off. I picked it up and saw my cousin texted me saying, "cous your brother dead someone shot him." At that time I didn't have any feelings in my body, because I have two older brothers and I didn't know which one. The only feeling I had was anger. Besides anger, my body was empty.

Then I finally found out which one passed away and I instantly threw my phone and punched a hole in the wall.

The first few weeks since my older brother passed were weird and depressing. The simple fact you won't be able to see someone you love ever again...you won't be able to talk to someone anymore...is just heartbreaking.

April 22, 2017, was when the funeral was held. A lot of people came. A lot of people loved my brother. When I walked in the door and saw him, he didn't look the same and I was waiting on him to wake up but it never happened.

My brother Lamont was eighteen, the oldest out of eight.

We had a close bond. I could tell him anything without worrying about anyone else knowing what we talked about. My grief has been tough because a big part of me has been taken out of my heart. It hurts every day, but I'm still maintaining. But that's still not enough to keep my emotions stable. I still feel angry every day, waking up knowing my brother isn't going to be seen ever again. I control this anger by letting it out in tears or simply by listening to music. I always feel stressed because I have no one to tell my feelings to, because that's been taken away from me. I have problems sleeping sometimes. I stay up till 4 a.m. and wake up at 8 a.m. I don't sleep very much, because I get nightmares about my brother at least once a week. I block out the people I love. I don't share my feelings about my brother with anyone—or when I do, I don't go that deep. But I think that's the main reason people who hold their emotions inside have anxiety or stress, because feelings are always supposed to come out sometime and not stay bottled inside.

The thing that helped me most when my brother passed was smelling his clothes that still had his scent on them for a month. The hardest part has been keeping my feelings inside and not having anyone else I can go to about anything, and not being able to hear my brother's voice or see his smile.

I don't like when people say they know how I feel about losing my brother, because I feel like they will never understand. Because they haven't lived my life. They were not there when I was feeling lower than low.

The best way I get my feelings out is to talk to my brother in my head or write to him, and it helps a lot.

The toughest holidays were Christmas and Thanksgiving. It was hard for me and my family because my brother was not there to see it.

Lamont's birthday is coming up. My mother is throwing a party for him, and she got a billboard put up by the street, with his face on it, that says, "Happy birthday, Son" from my mother to him. That's how we will be honoring him. I haven't put thought into the anniversary of his death. I know that day will be sad for everybody who loved him because that day in April everybody lost a special person.

It took me a while to get a grip on my grief because I was new to the feeling of feeling empty and alone, but I have been feeling the feelings for ten months now. I'm not getting used to it, but I'm starting to grow and accept things, because in the beginning I was in denial, till the funeral. And after that, till just a few months ago. My suggestion to others who have lost someone close to them is never block out the people who love you, because these people are actually there to help you. Another suggestion I might have is never give up on life because a person has been taken out of yours, because people die every day and you aren't alone and life will always go on.

I used my brother's death in a motivational way toward school because he always wanted me to do good in school and wanted me to be better than him. So that's what my goal is to do for him. In seven years, I see myself as a professional boxer because the best way I can express my pain is fighting, and I don't think as the years go by it will get better, but I will have more control over it.

Darius, 14

Little Derrick

WHAT IF

What if? It is a great question. "What if" questions put more logic and reasoning behind a certain topic, say my brother's death. For example, it made me think over the fact that God had allowed to have Little Derrick's life taken. I have thought "What if he survived?" "What if he committed worse crimes?" "What if he wasn't there?" The "What if...?" questions make me look at the possible outcomes, negative or positive. "What if?" questions also can bring acceptance.

IT COULDA' BEEN WORSE

It coulda' been worse. That has been one of my thoughts since my brother died. My grandma told me that, and it always made me think of "What if my brother's life was spared?" He probably would've had brain damage or something. It made me think God wanted Little Derrick to die because of more severe consequences in the future that could have affected more people.

OTHER SIDE OF THE STORY

Anger is a constant part of living with the fact that my brother is gone. I gained anger because of the news, FOX59. In mid-June, my mom texted me a link, and I clicked it and started to read it, and I shed a couple tears. It wasn't the article, but it was the comments of "but I don't have a problem with the fact that he was shot and killed" and "She believes [he] had every right to kill the teen intruder," and the fact that they mentioned his previous crime history, which was NOT relevant to the story. My mom walked in and told me, "Don't keep reading that." I got angry that night as soon as the door closed because that article portrayed him as a monster, menace, and "unhuman." Ya know, I just think they shoulda' told the other side of the story.

SHOULDA' DID BETTER

It's a lot of things I regret doing in the past and present time, but now I regret not saying anything to my brother for his last days. The common guilt of "you shoulda' did better" haunts me, shows self-anger, and made me burst into tears. People tell me it is not my fault, but that doesn't change how I feel inside. I always tell myself, "you didn't do your job as a brother," because deep down I know I coulda' talked to him when I had the chance, but I never did. I remember when he got out of jail, he told me, "Whenever you get the chance, just hit me up," which makes the pain grow. I now know that I can't make the same mistake again.

COPING WIT' THE PAIN

Through time, losing people gives people ways to cope or to deal with the pain. There are negative and positive ways. The negative ways of coping are drugs, alcohol, and bottling up. Positive ways are writing, staying busy, hobbies. At first, to cope, I just wrote one-word stories, like "Anger," for example. I would write the meaning, relevance to life, and how to deal with it. But as I wrote more and more, I ran out of words, and they didn't help. So I went to staying busy, which was helpful but made me develop a loss of focus. The point is that we all have different ways to cope.

BEING A FATHERLY FIGURE

Since my brother's death, I have always felt different negative and positive emotions like anger, guilt, motivation, and appreciative. The constant anger was because of the fact that my brother has children who are too young to remember memories with him when they get older. My brother has three kids. Kearstin, less than a year old, Amaris, two, and Derrick III, a newborn. I felt like Kearstin won't have the father who can bring discipline, protection, love, and support. Derrick and Amaris won't have the father to teach them discipline, support, love, protection, and manhood. Motivation pushed me to want to fill in the puzzle and do what my brother couldn't finish.

Elijah, 12

Poody

When I was six years old, my brother, DeMarieon, was diagnosed with cancer. He was nine. We always called him Poody. My mom gave him that nickname, so everyone called him Poody.

I think it was a weekend, on a Saturday. I was eating cereal, and Poody was in our room. Then he walked out and said to Mom that his leg hurts, and it started to hurt more the more he was talking to her. Then he dropped to the floor, crying in pain, saying, "My leg hurts." I was little, so I didn't know what was happening. I was just scared.

Poody's leg had been hurting for a couple weeks, but the pain would go away and come back. My mom kept taking him back and forth to the doctor, but it kept getting worse. After we took him to the hospital, we found out that he was diagnosed with cancer. Mom and I cried the whole way home while he stayed at the hospital. I remember him staying in the hospital a lot. I was so sad. He was always so playful, and now he wouldn't play at all, hardly.

He was on chemo for a while. I used to spend the night at the hospital sometimes. Other times I would stay at my mom's friend Tawanna's house. She was the nurse at the school we went to. We both went to Deer Run Elementary. I would be sad when it was time to leave him in the hospital, but I knew he would be home soon. He lost all of his hair during chemo. He would wear a lot of hats. He didn't like that his hair was gone, but we told him it would grow back.

The children's hospital gave him lots of gifts. He got an iPad, Xbox, teddy bears, and books. Sometimes he was too sick from the chemo to play with anything. He would lay around most days after chemo. I didn't like that he didn't want to play with me, but I understood.

He also got a transplant at Riley Hospital. He became very sick from that. I remember he always talked about his throat hurting from sores. He stayed in the hospital for a month. I wasn't able to stay with him at nighttime. Only during the day. At night we would stay at the McDonald House until my mom had to go to work in the morning. Then she would pick me up, and we would go back to the hospital to spend some time with Poody.

I remember playing the Wii game at the hospital with Jake. He was the nurse at night. He would come in after seeing all his patients and play with us. It was fun. I miss Jake too.

I was happy when my brother got to come home. We couldn't sleep in the same room, at first, because of the radiation. I think it was for a week. He loved playing Xbox. He played *Halo: Reach* 24/7. He liked us to call him Inconceivable, so we started calling him that. He got that name from *Halo: Reach*. Sometimes he'd let me play with him. That was the only game he loved on Xbox and wanted to play, so that's what we played mostly. Even though we beat the game three or four times, we always had fun playing it.

Poody had autism too. He would spin everything. And he would laugh a lot. Sometimes he would laugh at nothing, he'd just be laughing. He also liked to jump up and down flapping his hands a lot. I knew he was different, but I still love him.

He always wanted his own room, so Mom finally moved into a house so he could have his own room. I loved that. He would always put me out of his room if I was winning in the game. I would always beg to come back in. I wouldn't let him in my room after that.

We started going to a children's hospital in Cincinnati for Poody's treatments.

I think we would go once a week, sometimes twice a week. It was called clinical trials. I remember it was a nasty medicine he would have to eat every day. It was so hard to get him to eat it.

He would cry about it, but he would eat it. Sometimes he would get sick from eating it.

Sometimes it would be really early in the morning, and we would be on the highway to Cincinnati. We would stay most of the day. If we stayed the night, we would be in a hotel. Sometimes I would not go. I would stay with Tawanna if they were going to stay a few days. He did some treatment where Mom had to stay a whole week, so I had to stay over Tawanna's house for a whole week. I was so ready to come home. I couldn't wait until they came home.

My brother would always need blood transfusions. I wished I could help him. I would try to cheer him up by playing his favorite game with him when he wasn't mad at me. He started getting really mad all the time. I would tell my mom. She would just say, "That's your brother, and you need to get along with him." I would try to get along with him, but he was always mad.

We went on a trip to Disney World for Poody's birthday. We had so much fun. We stayed at a place called Give Kids the World. It was like our own home. It was little houses everywhere. Poody loved it.

They had a huge swimming pool, and ice cream all day. We went to Magic Kingdom the first day. We had a pass to ride everything first. So we were always first in line at every ride. I liked that part. We got to meet Goofy and the Incredibles. And we saw fireworks at the end of the night. We rode the water rides too. My brother loved water. He used to play in the sinks everywhere we went. We went to Animal Kingdom and saw lots of animals. We did water rides there too. We went to Universal Studios, and that's where we had the most fun. There were lots of rides. We went to see Bart Simpson and the Transformers. We went to Harry Potter Land. That was really fun. We got on a train that took us to Harry Potter Land. My brother loved it.

We saw lots of lizards too. They were all over the place. One came in the house and scared my mom. We got it out of there.

When it was time to leave, Poody didn't want to come home and I didn't either. We had so much fun.

That was the first time we were in an airplane. I started crying when we were coming there. I didn't cry on the way home. My brother liked looking out of the window. I was scared to look out the window. My ears hurt when we were on the plane. His ears did not hurt. He kept saying he didn't want to go home to the cold. He wanted to stay in Florida. I wish we could have stayed too.

After the trip to Disney World, my brother's cancer started getting bad. I would see my mom cry all the time. I would cry too. I just wanted the cancer to go away. He went to my grandma's house a lot. She lives in Fort Wayne. Sometimes the hospital would not let him go because he would have to go to the hospital in Fort Wayne. He would be so mad about it. Poody loved his grandma a lot. She would always want him to visit, until he was too sick to visit. Then she came to our house and stayed a few weeks.

My brother's cancer started spreading. He started going blind in one eye. He would wear a pain patch on his shoulder. There was a nurse who would come to the house almost every day to make sure he was doing okay. Most of the teachers from school came over to the house to see him. There was a houseful of people every day. He started not seeing at all and would just lay in the bed all day. My mom stopped going to work, so she could take care of my brother. My mom and grandmother would take care of him. He stayed in my mom's bed all the time. He also started wearing diapers because he couldn't get up and go to the bathroom by himself.

We moved Christmas up a couple of weeks so he would be able to celebrate with us. He didn't make it. The day Poody passed away, I was playing the game. He started breathing funny. I was scared so I stayed in my room. My mom, grandma, and Tawanna were there. He passed away on December 4, 2014. I remember hearing a lot of crying. I ran in the room to see what was wrong and my brother was gone. I grabbed the iPad and called my mom's best friend Eboni. She came to the house that night. My mom called my Uncle Deon, and he and Little Deon got in town a couple hours later. It was the saddest day of my life. We stayed up all night that night. Someone came over to get my brother dressed, and we got to sit with him a few hours before someone came and got him. I cried, I didn't know what to do. I had lost my brother. It was unbelievable. He was gone. I missed him so much. My mom was very sad. She kept crying for days.

A couple days later, they started making arrangements for a funeral. We all decided to wear blue to the funeral since that was Poody's favorite color. My mom made the obituary. Saturday, December 6, 2014, we celebrated Christmas. We had a big family dinner, and there were a lot of people over. We had a great time even though I wished my brother was having fun with us. I got to open my Christmas gifts early. I opened Poody's gifts too. We just never opened them.

I didn't know what a funeral was, but my mom explained it to me. I was going to get to see my brother one last time. We were picked up in a limo and taken to a funeral home. We walked in, and there were all these people, including my dad. I even saw some kids from school. I saw the principal from the school too. I saw all these people crying, and when I got around the corner, I saw why. There was my brother, laying in a blue casket. He looked like he was sleeping. I was scared. I began to cry. I didn't want this to be the last time I'd see him. We sat in the front row. I got to look at him. I was wishing he could wake up, but he didn't.

After the funeral, everyone came by and gave us a hug. We went to dinner with a lot of people. I was wanting to go home. After we ate, we went home.

It was very quiet around the house without Poody. After my grandma went home, it was just me and my mom. It was lonely. My mom would come and play the game with me. I stayed out of school for a week before I went back. It was hard to go back to school. I would cry in school because I missed my brother. I missed a lot of days in fourth grade, so my mom held me back a year. I started my other fourth grade year at another school. I really missed Deer Run School.

My mom put me in a program called Big Brothers Big Sisters. My Big Brother's name is Joe. He also lost his big brother. He passed in India. Joe told me all about it. He goes over to India sometimes to finish what his brother was doing, and that's build a school. He brings me back souvenirs and money from India. It's pretty neat. He takes me a lot of places, like to movies, hockey games, football games, and restaurants. Joe is so much fun. He keeps me busy. It helps me with the loss of my brother as well.

I also have a little sister now. Her name is London. She's one year old. I love that I have someone to play with now, even though she is little. I have someone else around the house besides my mom. She keeps me busy too.

I still miss Poody. There is not a day goes by that I don't think about my brother. When I think about him, sometimes I find myself talking to him. My mom had him cremated. We keep his urn on a shelf with some of his art and a blanket from his funeral that has his name on it. So I feel like Poody's with me. I know he is always here next to me. I know I will see him again one day. Until then, I will always think about him and the fun we had.

R'Mon, 12

Tyler

Have you ever had a best friend you've loved so much it's almost unreal? Well I have. I'm Claire, and I'm going to tell you my story about my brother, Tyler.

Tyler had just had his sixth birthday party. I was a few years older than he was. I was nine.

He had gotten sick. I assumed it was the flu or something, but it started getting worse, and the missed school days were piling up. I was getting dressed for school one morning when my dad came in my room and said, "Tyler is in the hospital—you're not going to school today." I tend to look on the bright side of things, so I wasn't worried. I expected everything to be okay, like it usually is.

But then, when we got to the hospital, things started happening quickly. There was a very nice lady who took my mom and dad, and my sister Emma and me, into a room. She told us that Tyler was fighting, but we weren't sure he was going to make it. That is when I got worried. I was shocked. It was like the world stopped and all I could think about was Tyler. I wanted to fix him, to make him okay, and for everything to go back to normal. We were all hugging and crying, and I couldn't think straight. I crawled into my dad's arms for comfort, but none was found.

I put on a strong face for Tyler, and my cousins and I went to see him in his room. I was nervous, but I knew that if I didn't see him, I would regret it later. We had to put on gowns, gloves, and masks. His cheeks were puffed out, and there were many tubes running all over him. When I saw him hooked up to all of the machines, I was furious. So upset with everyone. I don't even know why, I was just furious with so many people because I knew that Tyler didn't deserve this.

I didn't know much, but what I did know was that Tyler had a very rare disease. I knew that he had the belly bug, and that usually the prescribed medicine makes the bug disappear, but in his case, the bug traveled through his blood into his brain.

We stood in the hospital room, gazing at his precious face. After a while, a lady came in. She had tambourines and maracas and all sorts of musical instruments. She was very kind and let my cousins and me sing a song to Tyler. We sang two songs, "Don't Stop the Music" and an original, Tyler's favorite song. She put the original on a CD for us. It was emotional in the small room, so after a while, we returned to the waiting room, hoping for good news. All of our friends and family were there, and when I saw them I couldn't help but go in for a joyous hug. I felt so much better because this was confusing and overwhelming and I finally felt some relief.

I spent the day coloring with my sister, in the waiting room. She was eleven. Later, I got a feeling that struck my whole body with fear. Once I got that feeling, I knew I had to get away before the tears started flowing again. So Brennon, a close cousin of mine, and I went with my grandpa on the monorail to get some space. We rode it back and forth and back and forth. I was so stressed, but the soothing ride made me feel gentle. Slowly the day was coming to an end.

My friend's family was at the hospital, and they took me home. I spent the night with them that night to take my mind off of Tyler, but I couldn't sleep knowing there was a possibility he wouldn't make it. So I lay awake hurting all night, unable to move or sleep. The still night turned into a sunny morning. I was still out of sorts but hoped my friend's presence would take my mind off the whole thing. But I was mistaken and went home as soon as possible. I didn't want to look gloomy in front of my parents, but it didn't work at all. When I arrived home, my mom, my dad, and I sat on the couch feeling heartsick, and that's when I figured it out. I asked if we were going to go to the hospital to see Tyler, and my mom said, "Honey, he didn't make it." And that was the moment that I felt the most pain in my entire life.

I couldn't move, think, eat, talk, sleep, or do anything. I was frozen in fear and struck with sadness. I couldn't accept the thought of my best friend being all of a sudden gone out of my life. It was like a bad nightmare, and I was just waiting for someone to pinch me so I could wake up. But it didn't happen.

One of the hardest things I've ever had to do is go to Tyler's funeral.

I remember exactly what he looked like. He was lying there, so innocent, with his head shaved and his little body surrounded by flowers and stuffed animals. His eyes were closed, and that was when it hit me. He is never going to open them again. It was like someone stabbing me in the heart, and no one will ever understand that type of pain unless they are actually going through it.

I took a seat, trying to hold it together. I remember having to sit in the front row. My friends and family were there, and my teachers were there. I saw every single one of my friends sitting in the seats, looking very compassionate. I spotted so many familiar faces and several people I didn't know. It touched my heart that this many people came for Tyler. I remember the pastor talking about the gift of life. The beauty of life. I was crying, and I thought to myself, "the beauty of life?" If life is so beautiful, then how come death happens? There were pictures and flowers, and I was wishing it was all a dream, but I knew it wasn't, and I knew it was going to be a lot harder than I expected. I couldn't believe that he was lying in a casket. I mean, I knew he would be for the funeral, but it just became so real. I longed for one last hug, one last look at his smile, one last sound of his voice, one last feel of his soft hand. I wanted him back again. And knowing that I could never see or hear or feel any of those things again just drained me. It drained my energy and drained my heart of joy.

I missed him so much, and he hadn't been gone that long, and I couldn't begin to imagine how I was going to deal with this in a few years or so. What was I going to do when I needed my best friend to talk to, or when I wanted to play superheroes?

After the funeral, I was receiving lots of presents from friends, and I was getting hugs from people I didn't know. I got hugs from *everyone*. It was very comforting, and I needed comfort that day. I was hugging people left and right. Let me be the first to tell you, I am a hugger, and that was the most hugs I received and enjoyed in a day. But I didn't know how to handle all of this. The hugs, the tears, the feelings. It was so overwhelming, and all of it made my heart sink. And so I thought *it isn't fair*. Have you ever heard the saying "Good things happen to good people"? Well I honestly think this is completely false, because we are good people, and this is definitely not a good thing. Tyler and my family did nothing wrong. And I was so depressed because he died at age six and that is not okay. He didn't get to live his life at all! He had so much potential to do anything that he set his mind to. I had big hopes for him, and I still think he will accomplish unimaginable things in heaven. I expected him to be a surgeon or a police officer—something exceptional—and it makes me heavyhearted to know that I will never be able to see what he will become. And the thought of me growing up without him, achieving things that he can't, hurts me. It is too hard to think about me doing the things that Tyler will never get a chance to do. For instance, when I'm getting married, or when I'm going on a family vacation, I will think of him and how he doesn't get to do that. People say he would want us to move on with our lives, but what exactly does that mean? Do they want our family to forget him? Well I am never going to forget about my best friend, my brother, my sunshine, my prince in shining armor. He was not a regular six-year-old boy. He could take anything and turn it into something spectacular. Some days I would just look at him and think, *wow am I the luckiest sister in the world?!* He just takes your breath away.

And then I thought about my family and how they were feeling. I knew it couldn't be anywhere close to good, considering they have also suffered a horrible loss. And they weren't opening up, any of them. Not my immediate family, my cousins, or anyone. They didn't open up, and I wasn't sure if I wanted them to. But I was worried about all of them.

After that, it was like nothing mattered. I was still nauseous about the whole thing. Everyone was mopey and sad that Tyler was gone and wasn't coming back.

I lay on the couch with my sister, weeping for days, feeling baffled and heartbroken. Emma and I had to sleep downstairs for a few days because we couldn't walk past his room to our own. We went back to school like everything was normal, but I knew it wasn't. My friends were trying to comfort me, but most of the time it didn't help. Like when people would say, "He's in a better place now." Or "This is all part of God's plan." Sometimes it made it worse. But other times, when someone would come up to me and say nothing and just give me a good hug, it felt good.

There started being fundraisers, and people brought us dinners every night, and it felt bigger than I thought it was going to be.

Emma, my closest cousins Tessa and Brennon, and I started going to a support group. My mom and dad went to one too. I thought it was especially good for them because they lost their youngest child and only son.

Time went on and I started getting angry. I needed a reason. A reason that God took away my brother. I was trying to find someone to blame.

For a while I blamed the doctors for not fixing him. I didn't know much about the disease or what was wrong with Tyler. I knew he was sick, and that the belly bug moved to his head, and that by the time they did surgery, it was too late. That was the situation as I knew it. I didn't understand why the doctors could not fix him. That was their job. They're supposed to save people's lives. And they failed. They didn't save him, they killed him, and they hurt several people in the process.

Then I started blaming God. I blamed him because Tyler was the kind of boy who lights up every room he walks into.

Then, I tried to focus on the good memories. Like one time, Emma, Tessa, and I dressed Brennon and Tyler up like girls. They had polka dot skirts and long wigs, and they were so cute. It made me smile.

I realized that thinking of happy times was better. Like the time we went to Chicago as a family and had a lot of good memories. We went to the Bean. And we got good pictures of these statues of pants. One time we went to North Carolina and it was amazing. Tyler and I made sandcastles and played in the waves and had so much fun.

It felt so good to stop being sad and instead smile at the thought that he had a good life.

But everything was different now that he was gone.

After Tyler's death, our family became more emotional. Right when you think things are getting better, everything crumbles. Like Christmas for the first time without him. It was going okay until we kids got our stockings down. My grandma spotted Tyler's empty stocking hanging from the fireplace and started sobbing.

Sometimes I didn't know if I was going to make it, and other times I was perfectly fine and thought I was going to be okay. I found ways to cope not only with the worrying, but with the big Tyler-shaped hole in my heart. Here are a few of my remedies:

1. I keep a box of stretched-out ponytail bands in my desk, and when I get mad, I pull one out and pull it as hard as I can until it breaks.

2. Whenever I get sad, I play my favorite music and sing my lungs out.

3. When I get scared that something is going to happen to another member of my family, I hide under my

blankets and hug my favorite stuffed animal, Mr. Dickinson, as tight as I can.

If these ways don't work for you, then find others that do, because it's important to have a way to cope.

And when you are feeling kind of crummy, it helps to know that your sibling is being honored. For instance, every year on Tyler's birthday, August 7, we have a balloon-release at his grave. We also host a golf outing each year on September 12, the day that he died. We are also slowly raising money for a playground at our local ball diamonds in memory of Tyler. If you have lost a loved one, I strongly encourage you to do something like this. Find a way to honor them. If you think you can't, at least try, because nothing is unobtainable.

One thing that makes everything easier is that our friends and family, and even strangers, do all they can to give a helping hand. They sponsor fundraisers and meals and honestly try to do anything possible to help.

A lot of that support has come from my friends. They have really helped me through it. They brought me blankets and movies, and they had me over to spend the night many, many times. To this day, they still help. For instance, on Tyler's birthday, they will give me a big hug. And, with certain friends, we talk about Tyler's passing, from time to time. And to be honest, it helps.

I recommend talking to someone, eventually. It doesn't have to be every day or anything, but every now and then it helps to talk it out. I see a school counselor. I meet with her once a week and let my feelings out. She has stress balls and squishy toys, and she is a big help. She is really understanding and caring, and I want to sincerely thank Mrs. Cox for everything she does. I think if you have lost someone close to you, then you should talk to someone, and it will influence you greatly.

Loss is a tragic, difficult process. Some days I am perfectly fine and the loss doesn't faze me at all. But other days I miss Tyler like the sky misses the stars. I miss the way he talks and the way he laughs at his own jokes, and I miss the way he gets lost when he is dancing. I miss his hugs because, let me tell you, he gives the best, most warm, gentle hugs. He wraps you up with his small sweet arms. And he lays his head gently on your shoulder. He squeezes you just right to make you feel loved and special. And at that very second, you could just tell *oh my gosh, I love him so much.*

And yes there are ways to survive, but there is no real way to take away the pain that loss brings. Because when you love someone, you don't expect anything to happen to them. You expect to grow old with them no matter the relation, and everything is supposed to go perfectly according to plan. And I felt guilty letting my little brother leave this earth before me. Because I'm his older sister, and I have to protect him. I have to do anything in my power to let him stay here because that is what sisters do. And I feel furious because we were supposed to go together. We talked about it. We were going to play one last game of superhero princesses, and we would sit down for one last hug and go together in each other's arms. And he left early. Way too early for any of us to be ready. I mean, one day you're collecting tickets at Chuck E. Cheese's, and the next day your dreams vanish like a snowman on a hot day. Dreams are supposed to come true. Lives are supposed to be lived. Loss takes all of that away.

Tyler is truly one of a kind, and no one—*no one*—will understand this awful tragedy. Not even my family, because yes, they are hurting, but they hurt in a different way.

Thank you for reading my chapter, everyone.

I love you, Tyler. You are my best friend, and I will never forget you. Rest in peace, Tyler Jo.

Claire, 13

SUPE

Additional Information & Resources

About Brooke's Place

Brooke's Place for Grieving Young People is a not-for-profit organization based in Indianapolis, Indiana, with a service area that includes all of Central Indiana. Volunteers and staff at Brooke's Place work continuously toward its mission of providing support groups, therapy services, and community education to empower children, teens, young adults, and their families to thrive in the midst of grief.

Brooke's Place was founded on the belief that every young person deserves the opportunity to grieve in a supportive, understanding, and nurturing environment. This belief is built on the following principles:

- Grief is a natural reaction to the death of a loved one.
- Within each person is the natural capacity to heal oneself.
- The duration and intensity of grief are unique for each individual.
- Caring and acceptance assist in the healing process.

- Caring programs provide hope, help, and healing by giving individuals a safe place to grieve.

Since its inception in 1999, Brooke's Place has provided services to more than ten thousand individuals. In that time, children have learned to honor and cherish the loved ones they carry in their hearts and to discover they are not alone. Together, they learn to recognize, express, and embrace their thoughts, questions, and feelings about grief and loss. We welcome every grieving young person, three to twenty-nine years old, to experience the healing power of Brooke's Place. For more information, please visit www.brookesplace.org or call 317-705-9650.

The Writers

Claire Courtney Darius Emma

Elijah

Ethan

Gabriella Ramon R'Mon Zareya

Family Foundations, Funds & Fundraisers

If you'd like to support fundraisers relevant to those honored in the stories, please see the information below.

"GUNNER," BY COURTNEY

Gunner's Gift Foundation has been established through the Community Foundation of Morgan County, a registered 501(c)(3). The purpose of our foundation is to help other families who have children with terminal brain cancer by providing assistance and gift cards (zoo, Spaghetti Factory, etc.) for making memories. We currently have two families we are helping in honor of our sweet Gunner. For more information: Gunner's Facebook page is #GoGunner55, or contact Jennifer Burnam at jennifer.burnam@yahoo.com.

"J.T.," BY RAMON

The J.T. Randolph Memorial Scholarship Fund was established

to ensure that children, regardless of income, can have access to a classical Christian education at The Oaks Academy, the school where J.T. was known and loved. If you would like to donate in memory of J.T. Randolph, please contact The Oaks Academy at giving@theoaksacademy.org or by phone at 317-931-3043, or visit www.theoaksacademy.org/giving.

"JONNY," BY EMMA

JWL Foundation, Inc. is a registered 501(c)(3) established in 2016 in memory of Jonathan Legg. JWL Foundation provides scholarships to college-bound Avon High School seniors in Jonathan's memory. More information can be found at www.4jonny.com, or contact Sarah Smith at forjonny@outlook.com.

"KATERINA & EVALYN," BY ZAREYA

Fundraiser: K&E Butterfly Kisses. We are raising funds for a cuddle cot that will be donated to a hospital for use to give grieving parents more time with their babies who have passed, allowing the baby to stay in the room with the parents and in some cases even at home. We are doing this in support of Indiana Cuddle Cot Campaign. For more information, please visit https://www.facebook.com/KEButterflyKisses/ and http://www.indianacuddlecotcampaign.com.

"TYLER," BY CLAIRE

Tyler Joseph Williams Memorial Inc. is a registered 501(c)(3) established in 2015 in memory of Tyler. We are raising funds to build a playground in Tyler's memory so that his spirit and enthusiasm will live on forever. If you would like to make a donation, please contact chris@tylerjosephwilliamsmemorialinc.com or call 317-557-7390.

Books for Teens

The Beauty That Remains
AUTHOR: Ashley Woodfolk
SUBJECT: Life and love after loss

The Book Thief
AUTHOR: Markus Zusak
SUBJECT: Family

The Catcher in the Rye
AUTHOR: J. D. Salinger
SUBJECT: The death of a brother

Claim to Fame
AUTHOR: Margaret Peterson Haddix
SUBJECT: Family issues

Coping with the Death of a Brother or Sister
AUTHOR: Ruth Ann Ruiz
SUBJECT: The death of a brother or a sister

Facing Change: Falling Apart and Coming Together Again in the Teen Years
AUTHOR: Donna B. O'Toole
SUBJECT: Coping

Facing Grief: Bereavement and the Young Adult
AUTHOR: Susan Wallbank
SUBJECT: Coping

The Fault in Our Stars
AUTHOR: John Green
SUBJECT: Cancer

Green Angel
AUTHOR: Alice Hoffman
SUBJECT: Family

Grief Skills for Life: A Personal Journal for Adolescents about Loss
AUTHOR: Judy Davidson, EdD
SUBJECT: Coping

Grieving for the Sibling You Lost: A Teen's Guide to Coping with Grief & Finding Meaning after Loss
AUTHOR: Erica Goldblatt Hyatt, DSW
SUBJECT: The death of a sibling

Harry Potter Books 1–7
AUTHOR: J.K. Rowling
SUBJECT: Family

Healing Your Grieving Heart for Teens: 100 Practical Ideas
AUTHOR: Alan D. Wolfelt, PhD
SUBJECT: Coping

Help for the Hard Times: Getting through Loss

AUTHOR: Earl Hipp; illustrations by L. K. Hanson

SUBJECT: Coping

The Last Time We Say Goodbye

AUTHOR: Cynthia Hand

SUBJECT: The death of a brother; suicide

Looking for Red

AUTHOR: Angela Johnson

SUBJECT: The death of a brother

Losing Someone You Love: When a Brother or Sister Dies

AUTHOR: Elizabeth Richter

SUBJECT: The death of a brother or a sister

My Sister Lives on the Mantelpiece

AUTHOR: Annabel Pitcher

SUBJECT: The death of a sister

The Ocean in My Ears

AUTHOR: Meagan Macvie

SUBJECT: The death of a grandmother; coping

Rabbit Cake

AUTHOR: Annie Hartnett

SUBJECT: The death of a mother

Sometimes Life Sucks: When Someone You Love Dies

AUTHOR: Molly Carlile

SUBJECT: Grief; loss

Stay with Me

AUTHOR: Garret Freymann-Weyr
SUBJECT: The death of a sister; suicide

A Sudden Silence

AUTHOR: Eve Bunting
SUBJECT: The death of a brother

When Will I Stop Hurting? Teens, Loss and Grief

AUTHOR: Edward Myers; illustrations by Kelly Adams
SUBJECT: Coping

Books for Adults

35 Ways to Help a Grieving Child
AUTHOR: The Dougy Center
SUBJECT: Helping a child

Healing Your Grieving Heart for Kids: 100 Practical Ideas
AUTHOR: Alan D. Wolfelt, PhD
SUBJECT: Helping a child

Helping Children Cope with Death
AUTHOR: The Dougy Center
SUBJECT: Helping a child

Helping the Grieving Student: A Guide for Teachers
AUTHOR: The Dougy Center
SUBJECT: Helping a child

How Do We Tell the Children?: A Step-by-Step Guide for Helping Children and Teens Cope When Someone Dies
AUTHOR: Dan Schaefer, PhD, and Christine Lyons
SUBJECT: Helping a child

How to Go On Living When Someone You Love Dies
AUTHOR: Therese A. Rando, PhD
SUBJECT: Coping

Life & Loss: A Guide to Help Grieving Children
AUTHOR: Linda Goldman
SUBJECT: Helping a child

The Next Place
AUTHOR: Warren Hanson
SUBJECT: Life/death

Talking about Death: A Dialogue between Parent and Child
AUTHOR: Earl A. Grollman
SUBJECT: Helping a child

Talking with Young Children about Death
AUTHOR: Fred Rogers & Hedda Sharapan; illustrations by Jim Prokell
SUBJECT: Helping a child

Tear Soup: A Recipe for Healing after Loss
AUTHOR: Pat Schwiebert and Chuck DeKlyen; illustrated by Taylor Bills
SUBJECT: Coping

What about the Kids? Understanding Their Needs in Funeral Planning & Services
AUTHOR: The Dougy Center
SUBJECT: Helping a child

What Children Need When They Grieve: The Four Essentials: Routine, Love, Honesty, and Security

AUTHOR: Julia Wilcox Rathkey

SUBJECT: Helping a child

When a Child You Love is Grieving

AUTHOR: Harold Ivan Smith

SUBJECT: Helping a child

When Bad Things Happen to Good People

AUTHOR: Harold S. Kushner

SUBJECT: Coping

Resources in Indiana

The BRIDGe

"By Remembering I Develop & Grow"

- 8-week program for grieving children, teens, and adults; held once or twice per year in Lafayette, Indiana

CONTACT INFO: Dr. Heather L. Servaty-Seib: servaty@purdue.edu

Brooke's Place for Grieving Young People: Serving Greater Indianapolis Area

- Provides peer support groups: ages 3-29 and their adult caregivers who are grieving the death of a significant person in their lives; two evenings per month
- BP8: short-term grief support program in underserved communities
- Therapy services (individual counseling): ages 3-29, and adults who have children ages 3-29, who are anticipating or are grieving the death of a significant person in their lives
- Camp Healing Tree: summer weekend camp for grieving kids ages 7-17

CONTACT INFO: brookesplace.org

Flight 1

- Serves children 5-18 who have a health challenge, have a parent or sibling with a health challenge, or have had a close family member die from a health challenge
- Offers opportunities for children to build confidence by experiencing the world of aviation at many levels

CONTACT INFO: flight1.org

IU Health - Hope in Healing Pediatric Bereavement Programs

- Adults and children

CONTACT INFO: 1-317-963-0829

Out of the Darkness Walk

- Raises awareness about suicide; sponsored by American Foundation for Suicide Prevention, Indiana Chapter

CONTACT INFO: https://afsp.org/chapter/afsp-indiana/

Parker's Place Foundation

- Brings together parents who have experienced perinatal or infant loss

CONTACT INFO: parkersplacefoundation.org

Paws and Think

- Focuses on our at-risk community, both human and canine, through a variety of programs

CONTACT INFO: pawsandthink.org

St. Francis Bereavement Programs

- Adults and children

CONTACT INFO: 1-317-528-2636

St. Vincent Bereavement Programs (Indianapolis)

- Adults and children

CONTACT INFO: 1-317-338-4040

Websites

TEENS

2 Kids 4 Kids By Kids

kidsaid.com

The Shared Grief Project

thesharedgriefproject.org

ADULTS CARING FOR TEENS

After Talk: Write. Share. Always There.

A place where kids and families can write to their deceased loved one and share with family and friends
aftertalk.com

Coalition to Support Grieving Students

grievingstudents.org

National Alliance for Grieving Children

childrengrieve.org

Scholastic Children & Grief: Guidance and Support Resources for Teachers & Families

scholastic.com/childrenandgrief

The Shared Grief Project

thesharedgriefproject.org

Acknowledgments

Our heartfelt thanks to authors Claire Williams, Courtney Burnam, Darius Williams, Elijah Johnson, Emma Smith, Ethan Carter, Gabriella Einterz, Ramon Randolph, R'Mon Austin, and Zareya Rowinski—for so bravely and beautifully sharing your grief stories for the purpose of helping other teens feel not so alone in their grief; to the authors' parents for wholly supporting your children in this important project and for driving them to where they needed to be; and to Michael and Marcia Swolsky for your unwavering devotion and support of grieving children and families. Marcia, thank you, also, for contributing the lovely dedication to Irene Hoffmann.

Among those at Brooke's Place, we thank the board of directors for your support throughout the entire project; Office Manager Renee Richardson for always making everything so easy!; former facilitator Kristin Drouin, Therapist Joy L. Dyer, and Katie Hagerty at Camp Healing Tree for identifying potential participants; and staff members Carol Braden, Tara Ntumba, and Jill Pierce for your help in both gathering participants and developing the book's resource section.

Our thanks, also, to Brittany Cheviron and Kelly Petersohn of Healing Hearts Youth Bereavement Services at Community Health and to Drew Neddo at Big Brothers Big Sisters of Central Indiana for your assistance in identifying potential participants from the community. Our thanks to Central Indiana Community Foundation and Luna Language Services for providing comfortable spaces for our writers to meet—and to Sandra Warne for providing the homemade cupcakes!

And as we close, a special note of thanks to Butler University librarians, faculty, and staff for offering your expertise and support—and to Jeremy Solomon, Sean Jones, Masha Shubin, and Virginia Solan at Inkwater Press for helping us create and distribute this distinctive work of love.

About the Editor

You Are Not Alone is Dianne Martin's third book project working with writers who are coping with loss and grief. Previously, she assisted on *Tuesday Mornings with the Dads: Stories by Fathers Who Have Lost a Son or a Daughter* and its subsequent volume *More Mornings with the Dads*. She is currently producing a documentary film about sudden loss and deep grief. She teaches scriptwriting at Butler University and is the author of *The Book of Intentions*. For more information, please visit diannemartin.net.